ADVANCE P

Red Ca

"The positivity that runs throughout the book, even in stories that end on gruesome or eerie notes, is the best part: the sense of 'coming out' in many of these pieces is also a sort of coming to life, or a coming into the self. The under-current of acceptance despite the odds is pleasant and heart-warming. These are stories about kids finding out what it means to be themselves, and how to be with other people. That's good stuff..."
— Brit Mandelo for "Queering SFF" at Tor.com

"Eschewing the clichéd coming-out and coming-of-age stories in favour of fresher tales, whether cleaving to a quirky realism in 'Movember' or spring-boarding into the fantastic with 'Only Lost Boys Are Found,' by turns playful and poignant, delightful and disturbing, Berman offers a wonderful range of cracking good strange fiction for the queer YA reader."
— Hal Duncan, author of *Vellum* and *Ink*

"What *Red Caps* undoubtedly captures is the complicated essence of grow-ing up as a gay teenager. Cross-legged in the shadows of our closets, the world outside was a whole multitude of things: a monstrous adventure, a strange and unknowable universe and a place in which the grandest of villains could pale against the touch of a hand from the person secretly in our hearts. It's a grand achievement to have bottled that elusive feeling: those of us who are in those years now will find a great deal to cling on to in these pages, and those of us who have 'grown up' are likely to feel a heart-breaking chime of recognition."
— Matt Cresswell, editor of *Glitterwolf* magazine

"Steve Berman's characters walk a tricky line between youth and experience, South Jersey and the farthest reaches of the imagination. Even if you were never a teenager yourself, you will find yourself in these pages. Cue up your Red Caps CD, settle back, and prepare to be astonished, frightened, delighted — you might just meet the boy or girl of your dreams."
— Alex Jeffers, author of *Safe as Houses* and *Deprivation*

Red Caps

RED CAPS

NEW FAIRY TALES FOR
OUT OF THE ORDINARY READERS

Steve Berman

with illustrations by Divers Hands

Lethe Press
Maple Shade, New Jersey

Published in 2014 by Lethe Press, Inc.
118 Heritage Avenue, Maple Shade, NJ 08052 USA
lethepressbooks.com / lethepress@aol.com
ISBN: 978-1-59021-282-0 / 1-59021-282-7
e-ISBN: 978-1-59021-450-3 / 1-59021-450-1

These stories are works of fiction. Names, characters, places, and incidents are
products of the author's imagination or are used fictitiously.

Credits for illustrations and previous publication appear on page 199, which
constitutes a continuation of this copyright page.

Set in Agmena and Bilbo.
Cover and interior design: Alex Jeffers.
Cover image: Anonymous.

LIBRARY OF CONGRESS CATALOGING-IN-PUBLICATION DATA
Berman, Steve, 1968-
[Short stories. Selections]
Red Caps : new fairy tales for out of the ordinary readers / Steve Berman ;
with illustrations by divers hands.
     pages cm
ISBN 978-1-59021-282-0 (pbk. : alk. paper) -- ISBN 1-59021-450-1 (e-book)
1. Gays--New Jersey--Juvenile fiction. [1. Gays--Fiction. 2. New Jersey--Fiction.
3. Short stories.] I. Title.
PZ7.B45423Re 2014
[Fic]--dc23
                              2013042268

Do not thus afflict yourself, my good master. You have nothing else to do but to give me a bag and get a pair of boots made for me that I may scamper through the dirt and the brambles, and you shall see that you have not so bad a portion in me as you imagine.

— "Puss in Boots" by CHARLES PERRAULT
as related by ANDREW LANG in *The Blue Fairy Book*

**In memory of my wonderful DAULTON,
who led me on many an adventure.**

Contents

I

The Harvestbuck

I SHOULD IGNORE MY CELL PHONE'S RING.

I've already taken both an Ambien and a Xanax. With Mom's blessing, though she thinks I'm stressed and unable to sleep because I'm off to college at the end of the month. She doesn't even know I was dating Larent.

Within fifteen minutes I'll notice *things* in my peripheral vision. I don't know why it's usually curtains or bed sheets moving, even if I'm not lying in bed. If I struggle to stay awake I'll start hallucinating until I pass out. The other night I argued with a nonexistent wig. I think. In the morning things are never clear. But with the little pills I can sleep and never dream. Nothing's worse than your unconscious self cheating on you, behind your back, with an ex you swore you'd never have anything to do with again.

But the phone demands to be heard: the overture from *North by Northwest*, so my heartbeat races as the fandango quickens. Some days I want to be Cary Grant. Other days, Eva Marie Saint because she lands him. I'm not as suave as either — Larent seduced me by drawing a heart in the steamed froth when I ordered a latte from him.

Red Caps

"Yeah?" The crimson glow of my alarm clock reminds me I have ten or so minutes before goblins come out of the woodwork.

"Hey, I need you." My best friend. He sounds drunk. Deep drunk.

I think the door to my room just opened even though I know it's shut. But I'm home alone tonight. "Brent, now's not so good — "

"I'm lost. You're the only one I can count on."

That leaves me sinking in guilt. I've spent so little time with Brent this summer. We were supposed to do things, most of which I can't recall, but awesome-sounding things. And then I ended up wasting my days believing love was a cornrowed, espresso-eyed barista at the Grist Mill. A boy who I thought was bold until he drew his hand back from mine when I tried to hold it on the beach and who refused to kiss me unless no one else was around.

"Where are you?"

"I think past the Red Lion Diner."

I struggle with the directions even though they are simple. The Ambien has snuck up behind me and pressed a chloroformed rag to my brain. "Are you in the woods?"

"On the highway. Looks like Rt. 70. Trees everywhere. Fucking trees."

I know why he didn't call home. His father might be a forest ranger for the Pine Barrens, but Brent hates the man, so much so he dates girls not because they're pretty but because their families don't mind if he stays the night on their sofa.

I stifle a yawn. I want to let the phone drop to the floor and burrow into my pillow. But the bit of gray matter that's not comatose tells me I have spent the past week moody indoors and I owe it to Brent to go get him.

"On my way."

I have trouble standing. One leg won't compare notes with the other. I'm at the door before I realize I'm wearing only boxers and a ribbed tank top. I look down at myself, worry over how scrawny my legs are, and minutes pass while I consider if my boxers — too many stripes — are clean. That makes me laugh, but I worry that finding and slipping on pants would be harder than navigating my Jeep out of the driveway.

In the kitchen, I hunt down the instant coffee my parents swear by. Eating a heaping spoonful dry isn't so much to caffeinate me as to be so disgusting tasting that I can't fall asleep until I get some real java in me at the Wawa convenience store blocks away. The melting, choking grit is like the advice my driving instructor had — "You can't fall asleep behind the wheel if you've got your teeth chomped around it." Crazy, but true.

Red Caps

No crashes between home and the Wawa, though I drive like an old man, gripping the wheel hard and fearful that something will dash across the road — with the Ambien, it wouldn't even need to be real.

Only as I'm pushing twenty oz. of coffee and a tiny bottle that swears to give me enough energy to climb sheer cliff faces do I feel the cool linoleum beneath my bare feet and realize I don't have my wallet on me. Or my phone.

The guy behind the counter has either a really bushy mustache or a lot of wiry nose hair. Maybe both. Some writhe. Maybe as he's breathing. He watches me curse and pace. I may have mentioned to the walrus-man the Ambien. I definitely notice his gaze is not aimed at my face but at my boxers. Leering? Maybe. *Ohh,* I think.

If my parents ever caught me trying to flirt my way into free shit, they'd kill me. But I have no option but to casually scratch my ass so as to slide my underwear down an inch or so, while begging the half-walrus at the counter to let me have the drinks.

AUGUST DOESN'T WANT TO LEAVE, SO THE night's hot enough I don't mind driving the Jeep with the top still down. The cup of coffee is nestled in my crotch. I toss back the energy drink, which tastes like radioactive grapes, a good thing considering the situation. I throw the empty into the back.

Back in fifth and sixth grades, Brent's dad, Rick, would sometimes take us along with him patrolling the Pine Barrens. I loved how riding in his Jeep was like a roller-coaster, navigating the mounds and ditches of white sand and endless brown needles. It's the reason I chose a used Jeep as my first car.

The Red Lion isn't far. About fifteen minutes sober. I guess double that near-asleep. I turn on the radio. Loud. A man, hoarse as if he's smoked his last cigarette, is singing:

> *I got lost in his arms*
> *And I had to stay;*
> *It was dark in his arms*
> *And I lost my way.*

"I love this song."

Larent's voice startles me. I look over my shoulder and see him in the back of my Jeep. He's making out with someone whose features I can't see because

Larent has practically poured himself over the other guy's body. But I see pale fingers that thread through my ex's braided hair.

Jealousy pushes into my head. Anger, too.

I curse and the Jeep swerves. I have to look back at the road. When I glance up at the rear-view mirror, I see Larent looking at me. There's no guy beneath him.

Vanished. But the guy's fingers are still moving through Larent's braids. Only now they resemble thick maggots squirming.

"Brent's into bad shit. Turn around. Better to bring *me* home," Larent says.

I almost veer into the oncoming lane. There's little traffic after midnight, so the headlights aimed at me are distant. When I look back in the mirror, Larent's vanished, too.

Something wet and hot crawls across my thigh. I give a bit of a yell and look down, sure it is one of those finger-worms crawling up my leg. But it's coffee spilt from the paper cup. The edge of my boxers is dyed tan.

As I try to keep between the lines of the highway, my mood sinks lower. I was too demanding of Larent. And the fact that, likely, one day he will feel comfortable kissing another guy in public is painful because I know it won't be me.

Red Caps

ONCE I PASS THE NEON LIGHTS OF THE Red Lion, there's only pine trees. No street lamps. No one else on the road. The darkness is thick, the clouds overhead loom low, and the asphalt path becomes a tunnel. I start counting the somewhat faded white dashes in the center of the road to keep from falling asleep. I lose count often, though. I'm about as bad at math as I am at choosing boyfriends.

I find Brent sitting on the shoulder of the road, a patch of pale grit and dirty sand. His head hangs low between his knees, as if he's fighting the urge to vomit. I honk the horn. I'm afraid of running him down, so I stop the Jeep short. He gets up without brushing himself off. He's loping and holding a bottle in one hand. When he's close, I stand up in the Jeep, and ask him if he's okay — and forget to pull the parking brake, so I almost do run him over.

Brent's brown eyes are red rimmed. He's disheveled, white polo shirt and cargo shorts dirty. He must have been sloppy with the alcohol, because he has a boozy BO reek. Climbing into the Jeep, he mutters, "Thanks."

"Why are you out here?"

"It's my day.... Mom took the car." He sets the bottle between his knees. "She took her things." His hand tightens, knuckles become pale around the bottle's neck. "She knew it's my day and she left."

"Sorry, man." I put a hand on his shoulder. Brent's home life is all sorts of dysfunctional. Sometimes his father stays out in the woods for weeks. "My folks are away. You can kick back the rest of the weekend with me."

He takes a long drink. I stare at the bottle. The glass and label are still streaked with dust in spots. "Is that — " The black stag rearing on the label shakes its head as I stare. The tines of its antlers resemble pitchforks.

Brent does that drunk nod, both exaggerated and too often. "The Harvestbuck."

I'd whistle if I wasn't so drugged. And could whistle. "Rick's going to kill you." His dad *cherishes* that bottle. Brags how it cost a couple hundred dollars before Brent was born. Claims to be saving it for Brent's wedding.... No, that's not it. *Pledging*, that's what he always says. Brent's pledging.

"Dad came back. At least, he must been home late last night. There was...." Brent shakes his head, as if in disbelief. "He marked my headboard." He lifts the bottle to his lips.

He never would tell me what started the bad blood between them. But I remember Rick's descent into...well, creepiness. On those treks through the Pine Barrens, he'd be on the lookout for pine trees that had survived a forest fire. He'd tear off some of the scarred and blackened bark and taste it before marking the trees' locations in a spiral notebook — at first I thought that was part of a ranger's job, but when I caught a glimpse of his notes, I saw clumsy diagrams that resembled star charts or weird constellations. And he told us ghost stories, especially about the Leeds Devil, New Jersey's official bugbear, the thirteenth child of an eighteenth-century Piney witch. It resembled something like a bat-winged horse that could stand on two legs. The entire state has made a mascot of it. By our junior year, Rick had hung a map of the Barrens in his basement with red pins marking all the sightings.

Brent was one of the few seniors not to take the SATs, and his father refused to pay any college application fees. Rick swore he wouldn't spend a dime on tuition because Brent had a more magnificent future. I think Brent's whole reason for wanting to graduate was to defy his dad.

I start driving down the highway.

"Don't stop for anything or anyone." He glances out at the woods.

I laugh. "Not even a deer?"

He nods. "'Specially not for them."

We ride in silence a while. Every so often Brent leans close to me and looks at my end of the dashboard. I think he's worried I'm going too slow so I go heavy on the pedal. The pine trees on either side of us flow like on film. Flickering like old movies made with shoddy cameras.

"Where's the diner?" My words fill the gap between us. Brent stirs.

"This morning Gillian took me to New Hope," he says. "They have witchcraft stores there."

I should be seeing the gaudy scarlet neon of the Red Lion Diner ahead. But the road remains dark.

"I needed a protective sigil. These dreams, Sean. I see Rick waiting for me in the woods." He lifts a hand and waves at the nearby trees. "He's calling for me. He has antlers — fucking antlers! — and he's calling for me."

"Dreams can get crazy." I look at him. He's staring down at the bottle between his legs. I remember at school Brent took a lot of shit for hanging a beadwork sachet in his locker, but it wasn't full of lavender or anything like potpourri. He opened it for me once. Kosher salt and tiny bones. I thought it was like the *hamsa* hand my mother has on her wall.

I can't fight the yawn, but try to hide it by scratching at week-old goatee. The Jeep's headlights illuminate a figure up ahead, standing by the side of the road. Larent, wearing his Grist Mill apron. He holds up a cup of coffee, like he's hitchhiking — or offering me a freebie.

"Did you see him?" I glance back but if my ex was even there, now the night has swallowed him.

Red Caps

Brent looks at me. Squints. "I told you. In my dreams."

"There's no diner." I brake and drag the car through a U-turn across the empty road. The headlights sweep over branches. "I must have gone the wrong way." There's miles of Rt. 70 running through the Pine Barrens.

He's not listening to me. "Those New Hope witches are full of crap." It takes me a second to remember what he's talking about. "I tore a page out of one of Rick's books — I knew what I needed — but all they had was New Agey shit. Crystals and pentacles and zodiac crap." He takes a swallow from the bottle.

"So I went to one of the tattoo shops. Showed them the sigil."

Brent sets the bottle down on the floor of the Jeep and starts to strip off his polo shirt. "He spent an hour working on me." He fumbles. I find it distracting. Even more when he's bare-chested. His left pec has been shaved of hair and covered in plastic wrap.

I shouldn't think my best friend is attractive. That's like sweating over your brother. I'm thankful the Ambien makes getting a hard-on almost impossible.

Again I drive past Larent standing by the road. Only this time the walrus-man from Wawa is on his knees in front of him.

I taste panic. "Where's the diner?" I haven't even seen a speed limit sign to break the monotony of the trees.

"Fuck. I thought this might happen...." Brent looks ready to cry.

"What?"

"I'm stranded. After New Hope, I asked Gillian to drop me back home. I thought I'd beaten him...Rick. And so I was an idiot and broke open the cabinet and stole the Harvestbuck. I thought it would really fuck with him. I come up from the basement steps and the house is gone. I'm at the edge of the woods. The stairs aren't behind me anymore."

My foot leaves the gas pedal. The car starts to drift and slow. "No." I want him to be so drunk that he's slurring his words — I want to believe I misheard him. But he's not.

"I tried walking away but I can't leave the Barrens. I was sure if you found me you could get me out," he says.

"I'm seeing things, hearing things. None of this is real, right?"

He pushes the bottle against my cheek. I push it aside — I have enough in my system already, but he's insistent. "You have to toast me. Tonight's my night."

"I don't know what that means." The car's come to a halt, right wheels deep in the sand of the road's shoulder. When I put it into neutral, Brent grabs my hand off the stick and makes me take the Harvestbuck. The bottle is warm from Brent's grip and the top wet from his saliva. The whisky is strong, burns my throat while leaving a taste of old honey on my tongue. And something else. A coppery aftertaste like rare steak.

"So your mom really left?"

"Yeah. I think she's scared what happens next."

"What happens next?"

"You're like my best man tonight."

"Best man? What?"

I stare through the windshield at the empty road. I haven't seen another car since the diner. It's as if the world has shrunk to this one highway and all the pine trees surrounding us.

Brent tries to take the bottle back. I'm not sure why I don't let him have it. It's not much of a scuffle — I push him back into his seat and lift the Harvestbuck. There's kind of a wild grin on Brent's face as he watches. Instead of taking another swig, I hurl the bottle over the top of the windshield. Brent lurches. I don't hear the glass smashing against the macadam. It must have hit the sandy soil. It must have.

Brent collapses back into his seat and wipes his mouth with the back of his hand. I'm glad he doesn't go after the bottle.

After a minute, Brent says, "I know you've been seeing someone. Gillian saw you with him — a black guy, right? — at the movies."

My head feels even thicker. "Yeah. Yeah."

"Were you hiding me from him?"

"Don't be stupid." More guilt fills me. Larent took what Brent deserves. I lean over the gap between the seats and put an arm around Brent. His skin is both cool and warm beneath my own.

Brent peels the plastic film from his chest. He doesn't even wince at the tape ripping off. Weak light from the dashboard's dials shines on exposed skin. Underneath is the fresh tattoo, a series of circles and black lines. Fascinated, I reach out to touch. A slick of greasy ointment makes it feel like I'm not touching skin. Bubbles of blood smear beneath my fingers. Brent moans.

"He didn't finish the sigil. Told me he couldn't do the colors until the outlines heal. Amber and crimson. I really thought it would still work. Hoped it would."

Despite the drugs, touching Brent makes my dick stir. And I want him to stop talking crazy. I want to bring him back home with me, but why I want that is all sorts of wrong.

"Maybe.... I mean, I wonder if everything would have ended right if I was gay. You'd have protected me. Anyone who rushes out in the middle of the night to bring you home is a hero, right?"

Red Caps

He leans forward and kisses me. I'm not expecting that but I don't try to stop him. His mouth tastes like the Harvestbuck. No, stronger. This time I moan a little. For once, I'm in with the hallucination — I know this can't be real but I don't mind.

Then when I'm just about ready to believe it, he's not with me anymore. He pauses a second before he slams the Jeep's door. I think I see tears in his eyes but he doesn't say anything. He offers me a wave before he heads towards the trees.

I call out to him. Ask, demand, and beg him to get back into the car. But he doesn't stop and disappears among the black trees.

It takes me too long to get the Jeep back in gear. I steer off the road and follow after him.

Pine trees crowd all around. Branches reach over the windshield and through the open sides to scratch my face and shoulder. There's a path. I hope Brent's walking it.

As I make a sharp turn, the wheels kicking up bone-white sand, the headlights wash over a figure standing among the trees.

Rick's ranger uniform is filthy and unbuttoned. He's tied sticks to his head. They can't be real antlers. He's grinning at me. "Heard you like black boys, Sean. Come back soon for Brent — he'll be a right Jack of Spades when we're done with him." He laughs.

I tremble and floor the Jeep at Rick. The wheels sputter in the loose sand. He's gone. Gone but I hear his laughter behind me as I'm driving too fast down this little path. I pray I'm not going to crash into a tree and end up embedded in my windshield like a bug. There's the sound of thunder. Not a summer storm. I remember Rick telling us years ago how herds of deer running through the Pine Barrens make such a sound. Living thunder with countless hooves hammering the earth. I glimpse the backside of one deer, and my headlights make him look pitch black and as big as a Clydesdale. I'm thankful I can't see the rest of him.

There's no such thing as the Leeds devil.

I call out for Brent but my voice is lost amid the thunder.

I come to the edge of a clearing and slow way down. Brent's there, naked, crouched on all fours on top of a mound of earth and sharp pine needles at the clearing's center. I slam the Jeep's horn but he doesn't look up. He's found the bottle and keeps his head down, watching it spin on the ground in front of him like it's a kid's game seeking that forbidden kiss. The one he gave me.

I'm so focused on him that I never see the Jeep's still moving, faster now, or how the ground dips. The trench eats the front of the Jeep and my head smacks the wheel. A different crack than thunder and everything is night.

Red Caps

I WAKE WITH A MASSIVE HEADACHE. ONE

eye is sticky. The rear-view mirror shows that, along with many scratches, gummy blood from the cut on my forehead has filled the socket, but the orb itself is okay once I wipe the gore away. Sunlight streams through the pine trees and for several seconds I think, why the hell am I dreaming about a forest? Then I remember last night.

I climb out of the Jeep. The clearing is empty and the mound doesn't look like much, but the sound my feet make as I step onto the carpet of dead needles makes me shudder and I retreat. I spend fifteen minutes too long getting the Jeep to start and back out of the trench. Lots of folks sleepdrive after taking Ambien. I must have hallucinated everything.

But once I'm out of the trees and back on the highway I notice the bottle rolling around beneath the passenger seat.

The Harvestbuck's empty but a scrap of paper is rolled up and stuffed into its mouth. I'm curious but I don't touch the bottle till I see the diner.

At the counter, I tell the waitress I need coffee before she even hands me a menu. I unroll the paper and stare a while at the many lines, at the amber and crimson whorls of the protective symbol Brent wanted on his chest.

When the waitress returns I notice and ask for the red pen at her waist. I'm sure there's a highlighter by the register or maybe in the back room I could borrow. I start sketching on the paper placemat. I order a massive breakfast. I'm going to need my strength.

Most Likely

GRAY SKY, GRAY SURF, DIM HOUSE WITH GRAY *floorboards* — summer should be golden, not dismal, thought Roque as he peered out the window of the darkened rental at the empty beach. The scenery would be ideal viewed as a black-and-white photograph but experienced live it was a disappointment. Sheets of rain fell upon the sand and the air inside felt like gelatin, thick with moisture. Beads of sweat made his tank top cling to the skin of his back and sides. His swim trunks were dry.

Lying on the couch, one foot kicking pillows, the other wedged beneath the surviving upholstery, his younger sister, Leonia, moaned because the power was out, so no television, no telephone. Nothing that modern man had invented worked. Except the toilet. Not that Roque minded peeing outdoors, even in the pouring rain. "I'm bored," she called out.

"Read a book, Leo," Roque said without turning away from the view of the beach. Could the white froth of the churning waves mesmerize away a dull afternoon? Doubtful.

She lifted up the cold washcloth spread over her forehead. "Three days after school ended and you want me to read something? Raro."

Red Caps

"Then get ready for cosmetology school." It was a cruel blow, Roque knew. Back in their old neighborhood in North Jersey, girls didn't go to college but did hair. And gossip. Moving to Maple Shade for high school had offered new opportunities. Leo wasn't dumb. Just sixteen, so annoying beyond belief.

"I can't even call my friends!"

Her cell phone had been charging when a surge struck the house. Or the house next door. However electricity liked to travel. It fried her phone and everything else attached to that outlet. She'd then borrowed Roque's phone last night — without asking! — and drained it near death after ninety-some minutes of bitching to her friends back in Patterson.

He left the room because otherwise he'd start yelling at her, which would only annoy their parents, who'd blame him. Now that he was eighteen and out of high school, he had to be an "adult." When did someone hand him a pamphlet on How to Be a Grown-Up? Did that mean he should fret over money, like his mother, who had already bitten her fingernails down to bloody quicks because their vacation at Sea Isle City was a disaster thanks to ever-present storm clouds? Or should he be like his father and Uncle Manny and drink glass after glass of beer and lemonade until you couldn't see what cards you were dealt, so you started to lose hand after hand of Texas Hold'em.

He went to the bedroom — shared with Leo, unfortunately — and unzipped his backpack. He was the one in the family who liked to read. Thank you, Lita Sancia, he thought. Her eyes were bad, so when she had babysat Roque she asked him to read to her. He could never refuse her, especially knowing how she would praise him for being "such a smart boy" and then offer him a piece of hard candy she'd hidden in a pocket.

As he began pulling out dog-eared paperbacks, his fingers found something hard and heavy and slick at the bottom of his backpack. His high school yearbook. He didn't remember packing it...and shrugged off the mystery.

He flipped through it to find the page with his senior photo. He had spent a week agonizing over how to style his hair and brought to the salon three pages torn out of *GQ*. His best friend Charles always got a close shave. As the stylist hovered behind him in the chair, like a massive mosquito complete with buzzing from her razor, Roque chose a razored crop.

He smiled down at his photo then frowned at the writing beneath. His own handwriting in his favorite purple ink. *Gregg, I'll miss seeing you every day in class. And thinking about you every night in bed. I wanted to ask you out but could never find the nerve. Xoxox Roque.* He rubbed the ink. It smudged a little.

Gregg. Gregg Lehman. Roque had spent every day of high school mooning over the boy. And every night imagining what it would be like to hold his hand,

caress his neck, kiss his lips...and other, sweatier pursuits across Gregg's lanky landscape.

But he had not written this. Why would he pen something so revealing in his own yearbook? If Leo opened it — and one day she'd surely be so bored that she would — he'd never hear the end of her teasing. *Lehmann? He's Jewish. They chop off the ends of their bicho.*

He opened the book to the endpapers, covered in signatures and sentiments. All made out to Gregg Lehman. He had the wrong book. They had traded yearbooks to sign right after English, but he remembered Gregg handing his back, had read what Gregg wrote — *Never stop developing.* Too short and referencing their brief stint together as partners in photography class. Roque had wanted Gregg to admit his undying love and desperation at being parted with the start of summer. Or to ask for a kiss. But no, the guy had just smiled and said his goodbye.

So how could Roque be holding Gregg's book? A book with a message he never wrote. Roque began reading the sentiments from his classmates:

I thought you were kinda weird but know I'm grateful you loaned me a hundred dollars to get my fake ID. Thanks for helping me get wasted often!

I stared at you. A lot. All through Geometry. Why don't you like blonde girls? Everyone likes blonde girls. TV tells us so.

Dude, I don't even know who you are.

None sounded the least bit like something you would write in another person's yearbook. Not to a friend. He flipped to Gregg's photo. He wore glasses with round frames dipped down his nose so you could see his eyes. The photographer had caught him in mid-wink with a hint of a smile. Roque sighed, and then laughed at himself. Was he that lonely? No. Did he want a summer fling? Maybe. With Gregg? Definitely. And it needn't just be a fling, because nearly every kid from their high school was destined for Rutgers University because it was cheap.

Gregg's photo moved. Moved as if it was a few seconds of video trapped on paper. He dropped the book onto the floor. Pages flipped. The weak light from the sole window in the room must have tricked his eyes.

The yearbook lay open to pictures of the underclassmen. Juniors maybe. A red ink heart surrounded one girl's photo. Roque knelt down to read what was written beside it.

Red Caps

Sharon Cohen, who *owned* her frizzy hair and cat's eyes glasses. *I'm proud* (underlined a lot) *to be your only girlfriend. So what if it was back in 9th grade. We rocked!!!* (The base of each exclamation point was a tiny, perfect heart.) *Now go kiss a boy and try not to think of me.*

A notion tingled inside Roque's head. Maybe Sharon was teasing Gregg. Maybe... Gregg never ever mentioned a girlfriend. He'd gone to prom stag like Roque. But Gregg was a quiet guy, the sort who frustrated gaydar. There had been umpteen mental checklists trying to figure him out. Dresses preppy ($\sqrt{}$). Oblivious when he spills ketchup on shirt (X). Artistic — photography class ($\sqrt{}$). Takes photos mostly of girls (X). Doesn't know how hot he is (X). Borrows my music ($\sqrt{}$).

He flipped through more pages. Every salutation, every acknowledgment written by another student or teacher was just too personal. Mrs. Groolesky's *I wish you had an uncle. An uncle who had your looks. An uncle who had your looks and was a divorce attorney* made him laugh but Mr. Trall's *I gave you a B- because you're a heathen. Mark 23:37-38* left him ready to spit on the Latin teacher's photo.

Roque turned to all the various student clubs and activities, where the unpopular kids banded together for mutual understanding if not protection and the school's darlings gathered in shallow pools to reinforce their saturated popularity. In the photo of the Astronomy Club huddled around a telescope, Gregg knelt on the grass. Next to him sat Duncan Hall, the most notorious gay kid at Maple Shade High. Duncan whose favorite class was Gossip. A fresh tattoo on his arm, a string of numbers in blue ink that bit into the glossy page that could only be his phone number. And, below the photo: *Now that you've dumped that Cherry Hill brat, time to give me a call.*

Roque put the yearbook on the bed and began pacing the room, which seemed to have shrunk until its walls confined worse than any cage.

There was no reason to be jealous. Gregg was straight and Duncan was just being Duncan, all forward and flirty with any guy that moved. And Duncan *knew* how Roque felt about Gregg; he had told Roque not to obsess over near-beer, whatever that meant.

Roque walked back into the living room. He felt like his spine was a lit Roman candle, that sparks would fly out his fingers if he didn't clench them into a fist. His sister peered up at him from a book, a guide to winning poker, and then tossed the paperback onto the floor.

"What?" she asked. "So now if I want to read, I'm not allowed?"

"No. I mean...yes. Just don't talk to me."

"You're *raro*," she called after him as he went into the kitchen. But he couldn't open the fridge. With the power off, he'd let the cold air escape and his mother would howl if she even suspected something might spoil and food money be wasted.

He opened the door onto the beachside porch and stood at the edge of the wooden planks so raindrops would strike him now and then as he paced. He just had cabin fever. If you could have that in summer on the beach. Cabana fever?

Roque held a hand out to collect rainfall in his palm. Even the sensation of the cooling drops striking and pooling above his wrist, where blood rushed to and fro beneath the skin, could not distract him from thoughts of Gregg calling Duncan up, Duncan suggesting they take a ride into New Hope with all its cute shops and hipsters, Duncan faux-laughing in the jeep on the highway, Duncan draping an arm over Gregg's shoulder and, with his fingers, adjusted Gregg's shirt collar. Then, he'd stop laughing and lean in close...

Roque could feel a scream of frustration building inside his chest.

What he needed was to hear Gregg's voice. That would mean the difference between a weekend of complete misery and...well, something better than misery. He had kept his crush on his friend hidden and managed to remain non-miserable all through senior year.

Maybe the neighbors would let him use their cell phone. Roque was somewhat confident he remembered all of Gregg's digits. 7-9-5-2-1-0-6. Or maybe 2-0-1-6.

He ran through raindrops, crossing the space between cabins. The screen door rattled when he knocked against the metal frame. The interior was as dim as the one he'd left. A couple minutes later, a pair of round heads appeared in the doorway. Frowning round heads, one with shaggy brown hair, the other black and spiked with way too much product.

The teens blinked at him, as if suddenly awakened. A pair of "What?"s followed.

"Umm, hey. I was wondering — our power is out also — could I borrow a cell phone?" He realized the request sounded lame, so decided to add an "It's an emergency" to the end.

Spikey, the shorter of the boys behind the door, looked to and fro, as if expecting the flashing lights of a police car or ambulance just at the periphery of his vision. Spittle struck the rusty metal screen and Shaggy said, "No."

"Please."

Spikey muttered something to the boy, who then asked, "You the brother of the girl who's staying next door?"

"Uhh, yeah, why — "

"Rican girls are hot. So if she had asked..." Shaggy said. Both boys laughed, showing braces, as they shut the flimsy wooden door beyond the screen in his face.

Roque collapsed on the floor near where Leo read. "If it ever does stop raining, don't even think about wandering that way," he said and gestured toward the next cabin.

"Oh?"

"They're pendejos." And he told her what had happened. Nothing about the yearbook or Gregg though.

Leo giggled. "Rican girls are also trouble when we're bored." She dropped the book. "I have an idea. Grab a deck of cards and follow me."

Seeing Leo with him, the boys let them inside. But their smirks faded when she started demanding they clear space on the living room floor and bring over some candles.

"I'm not into any voodoo shit," Spikey said.

Shaggy, who might have been a year older, nudged his friend in the stomach. "Cards is tarot, not voodoo."

"Relax." Leo took the top card from the deck of cards Roque held. Jack of Hearts. "Just regular old playing cards. I thought we'd play some strip poker."

Every guy in the room — Roque included — let loose a "What?"

"Well, not traditional strip. You still have to ante up. That means money, boys. But if you win the pot, the losers also drop trou." She grinned. "Eventually."

Roque shook his head and held out the cards to her. "I am not going to sit here and play strip poker with my sister — "

"Of course not." She shoved the deck of cards against at his chest. "You're the dealer."

"But..."

"Confía en mí," she said. *Trust me.*

She stretched a moment, and the two brothers stared longingly at her. Then she sat down on the bare floor. Roque sat beside her, then the other boys.

"Texas Hold'em is the game." She cracked her knuckles.

Leo pulled out a wad of dollar bills from the pocket of her shorts. She unfolded one and tossed it into the circle. The brothers did likewise.

She didn't need to explain the rules. Cable television taught kids everything they needed to know to survive adolescence.

She won the first hand. The boys shucked their sneakers. Overpriced sneakers, Roque noted.

She lost the second hand and did not hesitate to remove her t-shirt. Her bra was peach and lacy at the edges. The boys' jaws dropped, as if the rubber bands attached to their braces had snapped. Roque looked at the hand she had folded. A pair of nines. It would have beat theirs.

After that...she never lost. A half hour later, the boys were pale and doughy and down to their underwear, ironically tighty whities for both. Roque estimated they had lost at least fifty dollars, plus however much Spikey's sports watch might be worth.

"So," Leo said, "I'd be willing to use this" — she held up her winnings — "to rent a cell for the night."

Spikey groaned and reached into the pocket of the shorts lying next to him. Shaggy scowled. "How do we know you'll give it back?"

She rolled her eyes. "You've seen my wanted posters? I'll tell you what, I'll give you both what you really want," she fingered the bottom fringe of her bra, "a long look — "

"All right!" Spikey shouted.

"If — and only if — you lend us your phone." Then her lips turned into a grin Roque had never witnessed before. "And you kiss each other."

"Kiss?"

"With tongue."

"No way no way no way," Shaggy said, but Spikey was paying more attention to Leo's hands slipping behind her back to reach the latch of her bra.

Roque stayed quiet because he was sure he had somehow stepped into some crazy television show and was waiting for the laugh track to commence. Or a commercial break.

"I want to see them," Spikey said.

"Dude, there's better on the 'net."

"No. Nothing's better than real life." And Spikey leaned over before Shaggy could escape. With one hand he grabbed a handful of brown hair at the back of Shaggy's head, securing the way for their lips to meet. Shaggy's cheeks puffed out, as if he were playing the trumpet and not kissing another guy.

Leo laughed. Roque slapped a hand over his eyes because he knew what she'd do next. He heard gasps, though whether that was from the effect of a first boy-on-boy kiss, seeing his sister's bare breasts, or C) all of the above, he didn't know. Or want to.

On the walk back through the rain, Roque stayed a few steps behind his sister, who had pulled back on her t-shirt but cradled her bra in one hand and the phone in another like a pair of trophies.

He was still in awe. "You learned to do all that after one read?"

"Don't be an idiot. Papi taught me how to play ages ago."

Inside, Roque fetched her a towel to dry her hair.

"Here." She pressed the cell phone into his hand. "You have ten minutes to speak to the mariposa that has you stir-crazy. The rest of the battery belongs to me."

Roque retreated to the bedroom to make the call. On the third ring, a voice answered. Not Gregg's. No, it was pitchy, unmistakably Duncan's: "Speak to me."

Why the hell would Duncan have Gregg's phone? Roque's insides trembled. As if he were on the edge of the flu. "Where's Gregg?"

"Roque Prieto! How's the surf?" A giggle. Everyone in the area knew of the torrential rainfall.

"Just put Gregg on."

"Still all moist after that one?"

"Duncan. Please."

"If I could, I would, hon. But he's not here right now. After sharing a fabulous breakfast together — well, you know how I leave men *crazy* — he drove off forgetting his phone. But don't fret — "

Roque hung up. He didn't want to hear details.

The weird yearbook lay open in his lap. But Gregg's photograph was now empty, as if he had ducked when the photographer clicked the camera. Or he was hiding from Roque. The original caption, *Most Likely to Hack into the Smithsonian*, had changed to *When I take a drink I become another person, and the other person wants a drink too.*

He tossed the book across the room and was satisfied at the thud it made, at the plaster it cracked on the wall.

Back in the living room, he dropped the phone on the sofa by Lo, who watched him move to the front door and struggle with the latch. She asked him where he was going, but Roque didn't answer.

He started running through the rain. He fell to his hands and knees onto the chilled, dark sand often, but picked himself up again and again. The beach was deserted and he was determined to reach the farthest end he could. And then? Then he'd just sit in the rain until pneumonia. Or the rain, which fell so hard it stung, would erode him into tiny pieces that would wash away into the frothy Atlantic.

He reached a line of rocks jutting out of the sand, perpendicular to the shore. Before he could climb over them, a car horn startled him. He looked over his shoulder. A Jeep drove over the dune grass, its headlights trained on him. He stepped aside.

It stopped inches away. The driver's side door opened. Gregg leaned out. "You're not supposed to swim *on* the beach." Raindrops began to spatter Gregg's glasses.

"What are you doing here?"

"Looking for you."

"Liar."

Gregg's forehead furrowed. "I drive through a storm to find you and I'm rewarded with attitude?"

"I'm not the one who had breakfast with Duncan! Was that his treat after you treated him to dinner?"

Gregg shook his head. "Get inside and we'll talk."

"No. I'd rather swim."

"You know I could get arrested for driving on the beach."

"Really?" Roque glanced up and down the beach.

"Honest. And I promise to be honest with you."

Roque walked around to the passenger side. He was thankful to get out of the rain, though he couldn't be more soaked if he had dived head first into the surf.

"When you're wet your eyelashes look huge," Gregg said.

"Duncan. Tell me now."

Gregg sighed. "Yes, I did go to Duncan's house this morning. And he cooked me breakfast. But I went there just to talk."

"'Bout what?"

"You. I needed a neutral party to talk to — like Switzerland."

"Duncan's not Switzerland. He's more like...like Hannibal Lecter crossing the Alps."

"That makes no sense."

"Nothing this day makes sense. I think I have your yearbook — "

"I'm not interested in Duncan. But he's been out for ages. You're out. And... and I'm not quite there yet."

"Wait...what?"

"I've always thought you were cute. Since we met. I was kinda hoping you'd ask me out some time. *I* couldn't ask because.... I mean, do two guys go to movies together? Hold hands? What are the rules? But then, you never seemed interested in me *that* way, so I just buried my feelings and was sorta content to be friends."

Gregg reached out and pressed his hand on Roque's shoulder. "And then, when you signed my yearbook, I realized high school is over and I won't be seeing you like every day. Even if we're both at Rutgers, that place is huge. And all I wanted to do was ask you out but I thought you'd say no."

"No. I mean — I wouldn't have."

Gregg smiled. "Duncan told me that you sweated me."

"He did?" Roque leaned closer to Gregg.

"Yeah. He encouraged me to go after you, told me he overheard you telling folks you'd be down the shore this weekend."

Roque mentally groaned at being such an idiot, such a jealous idiot, with Duncan.

"And here you are."

"And here I am. I want — "

Roque leaned forward and kissed him.

Gregg blushed. "Uh, yes, I wanted a kiss, too, but I was going to say, 'I want that date.'"

"I'm here in your car. You can take me anywhere."

Gregg was the one who started the next kiss.

"You really have my yearbook?" he asked.

"Buy me a drink and it's yours."

"A drink?"

Roque nodded. "I think you'd be a very different person hammered." He regretted saying it moments after it escaped his mouth. He didn't want a different Gregg but the very one that risked the rain for him.

"At one time," Gregg said. "But I'm really more of a coffee drinker these days." He reached into the cup holder and shook the paper cup a little. "It's not as hot as it used to be."

Roque wiped water dripping from his forehead into his eyes and looked out the streaked windows. "There's gotta be a pier somewhere close. We could share."

Gregg smiled and put the jeep in gear. "Would you believe this is sort of how I pictured our first date would be?"

"Most likely, I would believe anything you did, anything you told me." Roque's hand reached for the cup and found the heat of Gregg's fingers instead.

Cruel Movember

MY BOYFRIEND, EASTON, CAUSED MAYHEM on November first by arriving at school wearing a fake mustache. A thick, black-like-spilled-ink, bushy-like-a-worn-toothbrush mustache on his upper lip where there had been none the night before. I knew, because for Halloween we went to a party dressed as a pair of gigantic dominoes (my idea) so we could constantly bump and fall into each other (an excuse to kiss, also my idea).

Easton might shave once a month. He didn't even have black hair — his dark brown locks curled at the edges, especially the massive cowlick above his right eye.

But that morning he strutted down the halls. Other kids began chuckling, laughing, at his face, which didn't sit right with me. But he stroked the bristles as if he had been growing that mustache ever since New Year's.

Our homeroom teacher gave one look, grimaced, then asked Easton two things: *Why?* and *Please take it off*.

"It's Movember," Easton said. "Men grow mustaches for charity." He shrugged. "I'm wearing this to raise money."

The homeroom teacher, who lacked a mustache but had jowls, sighed. "Honestly — "

"Honest as Abe — "

"Abe only had a beard."

" — Honest as Einstein. Honest as Rev. King, Jr. They were proud mustachees." Easton adjusted one side of his mustache. He must have used spirit gum to glue it to his upper lip. I regretted dating a Drama Club boy. "The money goes to prostate cancer education."

The classroom erupted into laughter. Someone called out a lewd remark about how I must be in charge of Easton's prostate education. My face felt flushed, cheeks burning. More laughter.

Easton was sent to the principal's office after that.

I expected to see him in between second and third period, by his locker, without mustache and with detention slip. But as he dialed his lock, he still wore that...that thing. It looked even bushier since I'd last seen it.

"There's no way you talked yourself out of trouble."

He grinned, which made the mustache stretch its reach. "Movember's not something I invented. I showed Mr. Millar the website and he could not argue with my wanting to help a good cause. Did you know his uncle died of colon cancer?"

"Colon is one of those words I don't want to hear before lunch. Or during. Or after."

"Admit it: you find me extra dashing now."

"I find you kinda creepy. It's like I'm dating Stalin's son."

"Give us a kiss, Comrade Beau." He smacked his lips as if hungry.

"Ugh, no. No kissing while you have that thing lurking on your lip."

"Your loss. Maybe Comrade Eddie will want to play Gulag with me."

Eddie Wilkins, the other out boy at school, was the boogeyman Easton used whenever he wanted to make me jealous. Eddie was tall, gangly, like one of the test tubes he played around with in chemistry class, but never a serious threat.

Still, I didn't like to be teased. "This is a one-day thing, right?"

He laughed as he shook his head. Then he leaned over and kissed my cheek, but all I felt was the scratching of the mustache. Steel wool would be softer. That patch of my face remained itchy the rest of the day.

BEFORE FALLING ASLEEP, WE TRADE PICS.

Every night. Megabytes of affection. His that night had a close up of his mouth, lips exaggerated in mid-pucker, the mustache hairs looking like a forest.

I replied with a pic of a note. "Trim that thing. XOXOB." My cheek reeked of lotion to mend my tender skin.

NOVEMBER SECOND, MY BOYFRIEND HAD

traded the walrus-stache for a pencil-thin line of hair. Despite being infinitely less disheveled, the new mustache, with its suggestion of grease, evoked the same laughs from other students, the same sighs and eyerolls from teachers (though I suspected Mrs. Franco, the Spanish instructor, approved of Easton's new look).

"Better?" he asked.

"No. It's...it's something. I know. It makes you look — "

"Like John Waters?"

" — smarmy."

"Like John Waters."

He must have seen by my expression that the name meant nothing to me. "Creative genius behind *Hairspray*. *Serial Mom*. You've had to have watched — " He took hold of my arm. "*Polyester*? We really need to watch something else besides BBC together."

I like my *Sherlock*.

He took my fingers between his own. "Do you want to touch this one? It feels like a ribbon. A fuzzy ribbon."

"Do I have to?"

He let my hand go. "No. You never have to."

I TEXTED HIM THAT NIGHT: *IS THIS ABOUT*

that fight. We had. Last month?

No, was the reply.

October had not been just a time of silly costumes made out of painted cardboard. In the middle of the month, Easton became angry. Now, thinking about it, I see I made things worse at times, by kidding him about having "his period," but I didn't know what was wrong with him and I became exhausted asking if it was my fault and apologizing for whatever had gone wrong. I apologized for the sake of the world, just to break the wall he built day by day with clenched teeth, thick hoodies, turning away from me with clenched fists.

Then he broke a bathroom mirror at school. We had been standing in front of the sink and I kept him from leaving despite the bell sounding the next period. I had demanded he talk to me, and he broke loose and growled and raised a fist. I flinched — it had been years since I'd been punched (back in grade school) but I still remember the sensation of having my nose broken by a bully. But Easton

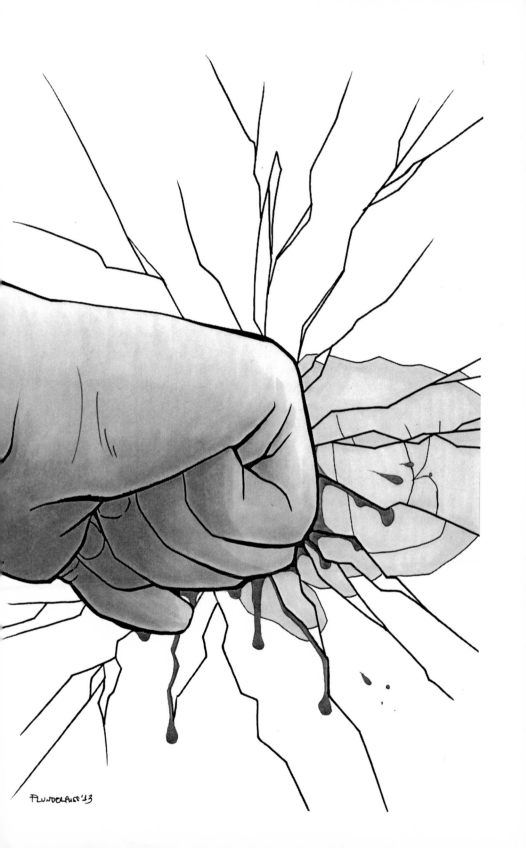

didn't aim for me but the pane of glass framing our reflections. The mirror spi-der-cracked. His knuckles bled. I walked him to the nurse's station.

That night he apologized and he told me he loved me for the first time. And the next day at school we hugged and everything seemed fine. Until Movem-ber.

On November third I saw the return

of that chasm between us. We had not kissed the last two days. Really kissed. So I didn't hesitate despite my repugnance for the black strand of yarn sticking to his upper lip. But I felt it, more than a tickle, its fibers snipping at my own lips and triggering a gag reflex as if I had somehow swallowed half his mustache. I think Easton could feel me shudder. I tried to hide by pulling away so fast.

"You hate it," he said.

"I hate it." I don't believe in lying to a boyfriend.

He nodded and went to class without saying another word.

And that night he never responded to any of my text messages. Or when I dialed him.

The yarn was gone on the morning of

the fourth. A wedge of deepest black, a smudge of nastiness replaced it. Confined to the groove of his upper lip: he had abandoned Mr. Waters for Herr Hitler.

More gasps than laughter. He was sent immediately to the principal's office. He slammed the home-room door behind him.

"Why," I asked him at his locker.

He barely looked at me. "Chaplin had one. Hardy, too."

If an inch or so of faux hair could menace, this patch would. It marred his handsome face worse than any pimple, wart, or scar. It drew my gaze, captured it, squeezed my heart as I stared. "Are you trying to get suspended? Are you going to show up tomorrow with something worse?"

I, of course, could not imagine worse.

"You wouldn't understand."

"What? That it's for charity? Fine, I'll donate, I'll pay..." I took out my wallet, emptied it of bills and offered him whatever there was. "Rip it off. Rip it off before the Jewish kids beat the shit out of you."

"Would you be with me when they did? Or watching?"

"I don't get any of this. Of course I'd be with you. Boyfriend, remember?" I flicked his forehead with my fingers.

"So being open and gay is fine, but this little thing — " one of his hands went to the vile mustache " — is wrong?"

"It will be seen as wrong. They'll think something is wrong with you."

"Maybe there is." He shut his locker. A kid passing by mock saluted and shouted out "Heil!"

I returned it with a flip of my middle finger.

"I don't want you bruised and battered."

"*Too late,*" Easton said.

I stood there and watched him walk to his next class. He didn't strut, he moved as if carrying some terrible weight.

I WAS ON THE ROAD FIFTEEN MINUTES later. My cell phone turned off in anticipation of the call I'd get about cutting classes. But I could not sit through three more hours of school while inside my head instinct screamed at me to do something, to save Easton. To save the "Easton and me" built up over seven months.

I knew his mother worked from home. So I drove straight there.

As I rang the bell, I had the sudden mental image of his mother answering the door dressed in a pink bathrobe and matching slippers, her dyed-blonde hair a bit askew, and a terrible handlebar mustache looming just below her pert nose. Something so wide that it would scrape the door, leaving a groove like a claw gone over the wood.

But no, she was dressed in sweater and jeans, face clear of any weird hair.

"Beau? What's wrong? Why aren't you at school. Did something happen to Easton?" The words tumbled out of her mouth, gaining momentum. I realized I should have run through an explanation as well as the entire conversation, in my head before arriving. On the spot, all I could do was say, "I just really need to talk to someone about him."

That did have the desired effect, and she welcomed me in. I followed after her into the kitchen where autumn sunshine fell on the table and a laptop surrounded by a cup of coffee, papers, and empty plates with crumbs.

"Want something to drink?" She lifted the coffee carafe.

"Sure."

"I can guess why you're here. This is about the..." She gestured at her upper lip. "Movember."

"Ugh, I can't even stand the word. It's not a month, it's a joke."

She held up the milk carton and I nodded.

"Many a true word is spoken in jest. My father would tell me that." She handed me a full mug. "Sounded Shakespearean. Like from *King Lear*," she said. Then her fingers went to adjust strands of hair that weren't really loose and in her face. "Sorry, I think Easton got his love of theater from me. His father, well, I couldn't drag him to see a play even if it involved stocks and bonds."

"The first one looked ridiculous, but now he's wearing one that will incite a brawl."

"The school did call me. And what I told them I can tell you and then you can decide how wrong Easton is." She sat down on a kitchen chair. She cradled her refilled cup in her hands like it was a small bird fallen from a nest. I felt clumsy in comparison holding a mug.

"We found out last month that Easton's father has prostate cancer. Easton won't even listen if we bring up the C-word at dinner. He takes his plate to the sink and drops it before heading off to his room.

"I don't know if anyone in your family has ever had cancer...there are stages, how large and how far the tumors have spread."

I took a long sip because I did not know what else to do. Or say. She had forgotten to offer me sugar and, despite the milk, the coffee tasted bitter on my tongue.

"Bill has stage three. So it's...well — " She let out a laugh that was almost a bark. "It's spread to his balls." As she covered her mouth, the cup fell to the kitchen tiles and shattered.

"Sorry, I shouldn't be so crass in front of Easton's special friend."

"Boyfriend," I said, as I helped her soak up the spilt coffee with a towel.

"Boyfriend," she echoed as we began picking up ceramic shards. "Yes, boy-friend."

I understood then what had troubled Easton so in October. Why he was so angry. And why he insisted on taking part in Movember.

I TOOK MY TIME DRIVING HOME. I NEEDED
to think, for once, and wandering through the twisted, quiet streets of the sub-urbs was supposed to spur me into brilliance, an idea that would ease me back into my boyfriend's arms, wrap us both in comforting warmth, protect him from what pain the future might bring. But found myself at the end wasting twenty dollars in gas and being late for dinner.

My parents forgave my leaving school when I told them about Easton's father. Then I suffered through a litany of illnesses their parents and siblings and uncles

Red Caps

and aunts and cousins had. Cancer, no, but I'd have to wary of gout and GERD and something else than began with a g that thankfully wasn't gonorrhea.

Upstairs, I stood in front of the bathroom mirror a while. Shirtless. I felt meek, weak, helpless, and I was the one who had a healthy dad. I closed my eyes, listened to the gurgle of the water draining down the sink. I almost fell asleep and when I opened my eyes, the first thing I saw was the cracked glass, the fractured reflection of Easton and me standing in the boys' bathroom in C-Wing at school.

I stumbled around and found myself in familiar surroundings. Home. Second-floor bathroom. Same old baby-blue trappings and shaggy rug. I splashed the cold water on my face.

I stared at how the water beaded on my upper lip. I leaned against the mirror. Fine hairs grew here and there below my nose and the water clung to them. My tongue went out and over each drop. I tasted nothing, I tasted like nothing.

"Please," I muttered and traced with a wet fingertip on the smooth glass two curved strokes above my mouth. "Please let me help him."

I don't know who I was talking to. Maybe myself, hoping I would listen, be serious, do right, for once.

NOVEMBER FIFTH. NO EASTON AT SCHOOL.

He had gotten into a fight after I left, had been suspended.

I had a black Sharpie in my backpack. Bought it at Target before school when the only people walking the too brightly lit aisles were sleepy zombies who'd forgotten something or mothers escaped from their kids. The pen was still trapped in the plastic and paper packaging. Coward.

I DIDN'T ASK, BUT MY PARENTS DONATED A

couple hundred dollars online to Easton's Movember account. Easton and I hadn't spoken in days. I didn't know if his mother had told him I stopped by, but the donation must tell him that I knew about his father.

I came close to yelling at my parents for acting without telling me. Instead, I thanked them because they were right to do something. *I* had gone to school with a single, stupid idea that I couldn't bring myself to do. But Monday...

I DIDN'T WAIT — COULDN'T WAIT. I DISCOV-

ered that huffing was not for me; the sickly sweet stink from the Sharpie cone-tip made me wince, an annoyance while trying to stay within the lines.

Red Caps

Sunday night, before bed, I took a photo in front of the bathroom mirror and sent it to Easton. Then, I shut the phone off. If I left it on, I'd check it every five minutes to see if he'd responded. I took Benadryl to make sure I'd fall asleep.

ON NOVEMBER EIGHTH, THE THICK MUS-

tache I'd drawn on myself remained dark. I waited outside of home room, trying not to obsess about how many weeks it would take to fade. The kids walking past noticed what I'd done to my face, yet I kept a calm shell despite all their many reactions; I only cared how one boy responded.

Easton came down the hall. Even from a distance I could see the bruises on one side of his face. He no longer dared the toothbrush mustache but a sad horseshoe drooped around both sides of his mouth. When he raised his head and realized I was standing there, he stopped in the middle of the corridor.

I took a few steps toward him. "I had a late start," I said and walked a little closer, as if approaching an angry dog. Or a scared one. "And I didn't know which mustache would look good on me. So I went kinda bland."

First one corner of his mouth lifted. He shook his head as if to clear it. Then the other corner rose. "Better than my last choice." He moved close enough that we could hug, but the hesitation between us felt tangible.

"I like the —"

And then someone rushing before the bell knocked me into him, just like what happened so often at the Halloween party. And he caught me and held me and we looked at one another and though he had what looked like a shaggy dog's tail hanging under his nose all I wanted to do was kiss him.

So I did.

The hall monitor broke us up, mentioned that he liked our matching look, but that we were late for homeroom...there'd be detentions for both of us...and to avoid cheap wax to twirl the ends. I twirled my fingers around Easton's as we walked into the classroom.

IRONICALLY, YEARS LATER, I'D BE THE ONE

sporting a goatee. Easton told me the other day he likes the way it tickles.

Thimbleriggery and Fledglings

The Sorcerer

BERNHARD VON ROTHBART SCRATCHED AT a sore on his chin with a snow-white feather, then hurled it as a dart at the chart hanging above the bookshelves. The quill's sharp end stabbed through the buried feet of the dunghill cock, *Gallus gallus faecis*, drawn with a scarab clutched in its beak.

"A noble bird," von Rothbart muttered as he bit clean his fingernails, "begins base and eats noble things."

He expected his daughter to look up from a book and answer "Yes, Papa," but there was only silence. Above him, in the massive wrought-iron cage, the wappentier shifted its dark wings. One beak yawned while the other preened. A musky odor drifted down.

Why wasn't Odile studying the remarkable lineage of doves?

Von Rothbart climbed down the stairs. Peered into room after room of the tower. A sullen chanticleer pecked near the coat rack. Von Rothbart paused a moment to recall whether the red-combed bird had been the gardener who had abandoned his sprouts or the glazier who'd installed murky glass.

He hoped to find her in the kitchen and guilty of only brushing crumbs from the pages of his priceless books. But he saw only the new cook, who shied away. Von Rothbart reached above a simmering cauldron to run his fingers along the hot stones until they came back charred black.

Out the main doors, the sorcerer looked out at the wide and tranquil moat encircling his home, and at the swans drifting over its surface. He knew them to be the most indolent birds. So much so they barely left the water.

He brushed his fingers together. Ash fell to the earth and the feathers of one gliding swan turned soot-dark and its beak shone like blood.

"Odile," he called. "Come here!"

The black swan swam to shore and slowly waddled over to stand before von Rothbart. Her neck, as sinuous as any serpent's, bent low until she touched her head to his boots.

The Black Swan

ODILE FELT MORE DEFEATED THAN ANNOY-ed at being discovered. Despite the principle that, while also a swan, she should be able to tell one of the bevy from the other, Odile had been floating much of the afternoon without finding Elster. Or, if she had, the maiden — Odile refused to think of them as pens, despite Papa insisting that was the proper terminology — had remained mute.

"What toad would want this swan's flesh?" her papa muttered. "I want to look upon the face of my daughter."

In her head, she spoke a phrase of *rara lingua* that shed the albumen granting her form. The transformation left her weak and famished; while she had seen her papa as a pother owl devour a hare in one swallow, Odile even as a swan could not stomach moat grass and cloying water roots. No longer the tips of great wings, her fingers dug at the moss between flagstones.

"There's my plain girl." Smiling, he gently lifted her by the arms. "So plain, so sweet." He stroked her cheek with a thumb.

She could hear the love in his voice, but his familiar cooing over her rough-as-vinegar face and gangly limbs still hurt. A tear escaped along the edge of her nose.

"Why you persist in playing amongst the bevy...." He stroked her cheek with a thumb. "Come inside." He guided her toward the door. "There won't only be lessons today. I'll bring a Vorspiel of songbirds to the window to make you smile."

Odile nodded and walked with him back into the tower. But she would rather Papa teach her more of *rara lingua*. Ever since her sixteenth birthday, he had grown reluctant to share invocations. At first, Odile thought she had done something wrong and was being punished, but she now she suspected that Papa felt magic, like color, belonged to males. The books he let her read dealt with nesting rather than sorcery.

From his stories, Odile knew he had been only a few years older when he left his village, adopted a more impressive name, and traveled the world. He had stepped where the ancient augers had read entrails. He had spoken with a cartouche of ibises along the Nile and fended off the copper claws of the gagana on a lost island in the Caspian Sea.

But he never would reveal the true mark of a great sorcerer: how he captured the wappentier. His secrets both annoyed Odile and made her proud.

The Wappentier

As the sole-surviving offspring of the fabled ziz of the Hebrews, the wappentier is the rarest of raptors. Having never known another of its ilk, the wappentier cannot speak out of loneliness and rarely preens its dark feathers. Some say the beast's wings can stretch from one horizon to the other, but then it could not find room in the sky to fly. Instead, this *lusus naturae* perches atop desolate crags and ruins.

The Rashi claimed that the wappentier possesses the attributes of both the male and female. It has the desire to nest and yet the urge to kill. As soon as gore is taken to its gullet, the wappentier lays an egg that will never hatch. Instead, these rudiments are prized by theurgists for their arcane properties. Once cracked, the egg, its gilded shell inscribed with the Tetragrammaton, reveals not a yolk but a quintessence of mutable form, reflected in the disparate nature of the beast. A man may change his physique. A woman may change her fate. But, buried, the eggs become foul and blacken like abandoned iron.

This Swan May

When Elster was nine, her grandmother brought her to the fairgrounds. The little girl clutched a ten-pfennig coin tight in her palm. A gift from her papa, a sour-smelling man who brewed gose beer all day long. "To buy candy. Or a flower," said her grandmother.

The mayhem called to Elster, who tugged at her grandmother's grip, wanting to fly free. She broke loose and ran into the midst of the first crowd she came upon. Pushing her way to the center, she found there a gaunt man dressed in shades of red. He moved tarnished thimbles about a table covered in a faded swatch of silk.

The man's hands, with thick yellowed warts at every bend and crease, moved with a nimble grace. He lifted up one thimble to reveal a florin. A flip and a swirl and the thimble at his right offered a corroded häller. The coins were presented long enough to draw sighs and gasps from the crowd before disappearing under tin shells.

"I can taste that ten-bit you're palming," said the gaunt man. Thick lips hid his teeth. How Elster heard him over the shouts of the crowd — "Die linke Hand" — she could not guess. "Wager for a new life? Iron to gold?" His right hand tipped over a thimble to show a shining mark, bit of minted sunlight stamped with a young woman's face. Little Elster stood on her toes, nearly tipping over the table, to see the coin's features. Not her mother or her grandmother. Not anyone she knew yet. But the coin itself was the most beautiful of sights; the gold glittered and promised her anything. Everything. Her mouth watered and she wanted the odd man in red's coin so badly that spittle leaked past her lips.

When she let go of the table, the iron pfennig rolled from her sweaty fingers. The gaunt man captured it with a dropped thimble.

"Now which one, magpie? You want the shiny one, true? Left or right or middle or none at all?"

Elster watched his hands. She could not be sure and so closed her eyes and reached out. She clamped her hand over the gaunt man's grip. His skin felt slick and hard like polished horn. "This one," she said. When she looked, his palm held an empty thimble.

"Maybe later you'll find the prize." When he smiled she saw that his front teeth were metal: the left a dull iron, the right gleamed gold.

A strong arm pulled her away from the table. "Stupid child." Her grandmother cuffed her face. "From now on, a thimble will be your keep."

The Message

DOWN IN THE CELLAR, THE STONES SEEPED

with moisture. Odile sneezed from the stink of mold. She could see how her papa trembled at the chill.

The floor was fresh-turned earth. Crates filled niches in the walls. In a cage, a weeping man sat on a stool. The king's livery, stained, bunched about his shoulders.

"The prince's latest messenger." Papa gestured at a bejeweled necklace glittering at the man's feet. "Bearing a bribe to end the engagement."

Papa followed this with a grunt as he stooped down and began digging in the dirt with his fingers. Odile helped him brush away what covered a dull, gray egg. "Papa, he's innocent."

He gently pulled the egg loose of the earth. "Dear, there's a tradition of blame. Sophocles wrote that 'No man loves the messenger of ill.'"

He took a pin from his cloak and punched a hole into the ends of the egg while intoning *rara lingua*. Then he approached the captive man, who collapsed, shaking, to his knees. Papa blew into one hole and a vapor reeking of sulfur drifted out to surround the messenger. Screams turned into the frantic call of a songbird.

"We'll send him back to the prince in a gilded cage with a message. 'We delightfully accept your offer of an engagement ball.' Perhaps I should have turned him into a parrot and he could have spoken that."

"Papa," Odile chided.

"I'll return his form after the wedding. I promise." He carried the egg to one shelf and pulled out the crate of curse eggs nestled in soil. "What king more wisely cares for his subjects?"

The Prince

THE PRINCE WOULD HAVE RATHER MUCKED

out every filthy stall in every stable of the kingdom than announce his engagement to the sorcerer's daughter at the ball. His father must have schemed his downfall; why else condemn him to marry a harpy?

"Father, be reasonable. Why not the Duke of Bremen's daughter?" The prince glanced up at the fake sky the guildsmen were painting on the ballroom's ceiling. A cloud appeared with a brushstroke.

"The one so lovely that her parents keep her at a cloister?" asked the king. "Boy, your wife should be faithful only to you. Should she look higher to God, she'll never pay you any respect."

"Then that Countess from Schaumberg —"

The king sighed. "Son, there are many fine lands with many fine daughters but none of them have magic."

"Parlor tricks!"

"Being turned into a turkey is not a trick. Besides, von Rothbart is the most learned man I have ever met. If his daughter has half the mind, half the talent..."

"Speaking dead languages and reciting dusty verse won't keep a kingdom." The king laughed. "Don't tell that to Cardinal Passerine."

The Fledgling

IN THE SILENCE, ODILE LOOKED UP FROM yellowed pages that told how a pelican's brood are stillborn until the mother pecks her chest and resurrects them with her own blood. Odile had no memory of her own mother. Papa would never answer any question she asked about her.

She pinched the flame out in the sconce's candle and opened the shutters. The outside night had so many intriguing sounds. Even if she only listened to the breeze it would be enough to entice her from her room.

She went to her dresser, opened the last drawer, and found underneath old mohair sweaters the last of the golden wappentier eggs she had taken. She could break it now, turn herself into a night bird and fly free. The thought tempted her as she stared at her own weak reflection on the shell. She polished it for a moment against her dressing gown.

But the need to see Elster's face overpowered her.

So, as she had done so many nights, Odile gathered and tied bed sheets and old clothes together as a makeshift rope to climb down the outer walls of her papa's tower.

As she descended, guided only by moonlight, something large flew near her head. Odile became still, with the egg safe in a makeshift sling around her chest, her toes squeezing past crumbling mortar. A fledermaus? Her papa called them vermin; he hunted them as the pother owl. If he should spot her.... But no, she did not hear his voice demand she return to her room. Perhaps it was the wappentier. Still clinging to the wall, she waited for the world to end, as her papa had said would happen if the great bird ever escaped from its cage. But her heartbeat slowly calmed and she became embarrassed by all her fears. The elder von Rothbart would have fallen asleep at his desk, cheek smearing ink on the page. The sad wappentier would be huddled behind strong bars. Perhaps it also dreamed of freedom.

Once on the ground, Odile walked toward the moat. Sleeping swans rested on the bank. Their long necks twisted back and their bills tucked into pristine feathers.

She held up the wappentier egg. Words of *rara lingua* altered her fingernail, making it sharp as a knife. She punctured the two holes, and as she blew into the first, her thoughts were full of incantations and her love's name. She had trouble holding the words in her head, as if alive and caged, they wanted release on the tongue. Maybe Papa could not stop from turning men into birds, though Odile suspected he truly enjoyed doing so.

She never tired of watching the albumen sputter out of the shell and drift over the quiet swans like marsh fire before falling like gold rain onto one in their midst.

Elster stretched pale limbs. Odile thought the maid looked like some unearthly flower slipping along the damp bank, unfurling slender arms and long blonde hair. Then she stumbled until Odile took her by the hand and offered calm words while the shock of the transformation diminished.

They fled into the woods. Elster laughed to run again. She stopped to reach for fallen leaves, touch bark, then pull at a loose thread of Odile's dressing gown and smile.

Elster had been brought to the tower to fashion Odile a dress for court. Odile could remember that first afternoon, when she had been standing on a chair while the most beautiful girl she'd ever seen stretched and knelt below her measuring. Odile had never felt so awkward, sure that she'd topple at any moment, yet so ethereal, confident that if she slipped, she would glide to the floor.

Papa instructed Elster that Odile's gown was to be fashioned from sticks and string, like a proper bird's nest. But, alone together, Elster showed Odile bolts of silk and linen, guiding her hand along the cloth to feel its softness. She would reveal strands of chocolate-colored ribbon and thread them through Odile's hair while whispering how pretty she could be. Her lips had lightly brushed Odile's ears.

When Papa barged into Odile's room and found the rushes and leaves abandoned at their feet and a luxurious gown in Elster's lap, he dragged Elster down to the cellar. A tearful Odile followed, but she could not find the voice to beg him not to use a rotten wappentier egg.

In the woods, they stopped, breathless, against a tree trunk. "I brought you a present," Odile said.

"A coach that will carry us far away from your father?"

Odile shook her head. She unlaced the high top of her dressing gown and allowed the neckline to slip down inches. She wore the prince's bribe but now lifted it off her neck. The thick gold links, the amethysts like frozen drops of wine, seemed to catch the moon's fancy as much as their own.

"This must be worth a fortune." Elster stroked the necklace Odile draped over her long, smooth neck.

"Perhaps. Come morning, I would like to know which swan is you by this."

Elster took a step away from Odile. Then another until the tree was between them. "Another day trapped. And another. And when you marry the prince, what of me? No one will come for me then."

"Papa says he will release all of you. Besides, I don't want to marry the prince."

"No. I see every morning as a swan. You can't — won't — refuse your father."

Odile sighed. Lately, she found herself daydreaming that Papa had found her as a chick, fallen from the nest, and turned her into a child. "I've never seen the prince," Odile said as she began climbing the tree.

"He'll be handsome. An expensive uniform with shining medals and epaulets. That will make him handsome."

"I heard his father and mother are siblings. He probably has six fingers on a hand." Odile reached down from the fat branch she sat upon to pull Elster up beside her.

"Better to hold you with."

"The ball is tomorrow night."

"What did he do with the gown I made you?"

"He told me to burn it. I showed him the ashes of an apron. It's hidden beneath my bed."

"Let me wear it. Let me come along to the ball with you."

"You would want to see me dance with him?"

Elster threaded her fingers through Odile's hair, sweeping a twig from the ends. "Wouldn't you rather I be there than your father?"

Odile leaned close to Elster and marveled at how soft her skin felt. Her pale cheeks. Her arms, her thighs. Odile wanted music then, for them to dance together dangerously on the branches. Balls and courts and gowns seemed destined for other girls.

The Coach

ON THE NIGHT OF THE BALL, VON ROTHBART surprised Odile with a coach and driver. "I returned some lost sons and daughters we had around the tower for the reward." He patted the rosewood sides of the coach. "I imagine you'll be traveling to and from the palace in the days to come. A princess shouldn't be flying."

Odile opened the door and looked inside. The seats were plush and satin.

"You wear the same expression as the last man I put in the cellar cage." He kissed her cheek. "Would a life of means and comfort be so horrible?"

The words in her head failed Odile. They wouldn't arrange themselves in an explanation, in the right order to convey to Papa her worries about leaving the tower, her disgust at having to marry a man she didn't know and could never care for. Instead she pressed herself against him. The bound twigs at her bosom stabbed her chest. The only thing that kept her from crying was the golden egg she had secreted in the nest gown she wore.

When the coach reached the woods, Odile shouted for the driver to stop. He looked nervous when she opened the door and stepped out on to the road.

"Fräulein, your father insisted you arrive tonight. He said I'd be eatin' worms for the rest of my days."

"A moment." She had difficulty running, because of the rigid gown. She knew her knees would be scratched raw by the time she reached the swans. Odile guided a transformed Elster to the road. The sight of the magnificent coach roused her from the change's fugue.

"Finally I ride with style." Elster waited for the driver to help her climb the small steps into the coach. "But I have no dress to wear tonight."

Odile sat down beside her and stroked the curtains and the cushions. "There is fabric wasted here to make ten gowns."

When Odile transformed her fingernails to sharp points to rip free satin and gauze, she noticed Elster inch away. The magic frightened her. Odile offered a smile and her hand to use as needles. Elster took hold of her wrist with an almost cautious touch.

The bodice took shape in Elster's lap. "We could stay on the road. Not even go to the ball. You could turn the driver into a red-breasted robin and we could go wherever we want."

"I've never been this far away from home." Odile wondered why she hadn't considered such an escape. But all her thoughts had been filled with the dreaded ball, as if she had no choice but to accept the prince's hand. She glanced out the tiny window at the world rushing past. But Papa would be waiting for her tonight. There would be studies tomorrow and feeding the wappentier, and she couldn't abandon Papa.

It was a relief that she had no black egg with her, that she had no means to turn a man into fowl. She had never done so, could not imagine the need. So she shook her head.

Elster frowned. "Always your father's girl." She reached down and bit free the thread linking Odile's fingers and her gown. "Remember that I offered you a choice."

The Ball

THE PALACE BALLROOM HAD BEEN TRANS-
formed into an enchanting wood. The rugs from distant Persia rolled up to allow space for hundreds of fallen leaves fashioned from silk. The noble attendees slipped on the leaves often. A white-bearded ambassador from Lombardy fell and broke his hip; when carried off he claimed it was no accident but an *atto di guerra*.

Trees fashioned by carpenters and blacksmiths spread along the walls. The head cook had sculpted dough songbirds, encrusted them with dyed sugars and added marzipan beaks.

The orchestra was instructed not to play any tune not found in nature. This left them perplexed and often silent.

"Fräulein Odile von Rothbart and her guest Fräulein Elster Schwanensee." The herald standing on the landing had an oiled, thick mustache.

Odile cringed beneath the layers of twigs and parchment that covered her torso and trailed off to sweep the floor. How they all stared at her. She wanted to squeeze Elster's hand for strength but found nothing in her grasp; she paused halfway down the staircase, perplexed by her empty hand. She turned back to the crowd of courtiers but saw no sign of her swan maid.

The courtiers flocked around her. They chattered, so many voices that she had trouble understanding anything they said.

"That frock is so...unusual." The elderly man who spoke wore a cardinal's red robes. "How very bold to be so...indigenous."

A sharp-nosed matron held a silken pomander beneath her nostrils. "I hope that is imported mud binding those sticks," she muttered.

The Lovebirds

ELSTER PICKED UP A CRYSTAL GLASS OF
chilled Silvaner from a servant's platter. She held the dry wine long in her mouth, wanting to remember its taste when she had to plunge a beak into moat water.

"Fräulein von Rothbart. Our fathers would have us dance."

Elster turned around. She had been right about the uniform. Her heart ached to touch the dark blue-like-evening wool, the gilded buttons, the medals at the chest, and the thick gold braid on the shoulders. A uniform like that would only be at home in a wardrobe filled with fur-lined coats, jodhpurs for riding with leather boots, silken smoking jackets that smelled of Turkish tobacco. The man who owned such clothes would only be satisfied if his darling matched him in taste.

She lowered her gaze with much flutter and curtsied low.

"I am pleased you wore my gift." The prince had trimmed fingernails that looked so pink as to possibly be polished. He lifted up one section of the necklace she wore. The tip of his pinky slid into the crease between her breasts. "How else would I know you?"

She offered a promissory smile.

He led her near where the musicians sought to emulate the chirp of crickets at dusk.

"So, I must remember to commend your father on his most successful enchantment."

"Your Imperial and Royal Highness is too kind."

Three other couples, lavish in expensive fabric and pearls and silver, joined them in a quadrille. As the pairs moved, their feet kicked up plumes of silk leaves. Despite the gold she wore around her neck, Elster felt as if she were a tarnished coin thimblerigged along the dance floor.

"I have an admission to make," she whispered in the prince's ear when next she passed him. "I'm not the sorcerer's daughter."

The prince took hold of her arm, not in a rough grasp, but as if afraid she would vanish. "If this is a trick — "

"Once I shared your life of comfort. Sheets as soft as a sigh. Banquet halls filled with drink and laughter. Never the need for a seamstress as I never wore a dress twice.

"My parents were vassals in Saxony. Long dead now." She slipped free of his hold and went to the nearest window. She waited for his footsteps, waited to feel him press against her. "Am I looking east? To a lost home?"

She turned around. Her eyes lingered a moment on the plum-colored ribbon sewn to one medal on his chest. "So many years ago — I have lost count — a demonic bird flew into my bedchamber."

"Von Rothbart."

Elster nodded at his disgust. "He stole me away, back to his lonely tower. Every morning I woke to find myself trapped as a swan. Every night he demands I become his bride. I have always refused."

"I have never stood before such virtue." The prince began to tear as he stepped back and then fell to one knee. "Though I can see why even the Devil would promise himself to you."

His eyes looked too shiny, as if he might start crying or raving like a madman. Elster had seen the same sheen in Odile's eyes. Elster squeezed the prince's hand

but looked over her shoulder at where she had parted from the sorcerer's daughter. The art of turning someone into a bird would never dress her in cashmere or damask. Feathers were only so soft and comforting.

The Lost

WHEN ODILE WAS A YOUNGER GIRL, HER father told her terrible tales every *Abend vor Allerheiligen*. One had been about an insane cook who had trapped over twenty blackbirds and half-cooked them as part of a pie. All for the delight of a royal court. Odile had nightmares about being trapped with screeching chicks, all cramped in the dark, the stink of dough, the rising heat. She would not eat any pastry for years.

Watching Elster dance with the prince filled Odile with pain. She didn't know whether such hurt needed tears or screams to be freed. She approached them. The pair stopped turning.

"Your warning in the coach? Is this your choice?" asked Odile. Elster nodded though her hands released the prince's neck.

The *rara lingua* to tear the swan maid's humanity from her slipped between Odile's lips with one long gasp. Her face felt feverish and damp. Perhaps tears. She called for Papa to take the swan by the legs into the kitchen and return carrying a bulging strudel for the prince.

The Strygian

AS A LONG-EARED POTHER OWL, VON Rothbart had hoped to intimidate the nobles with a blood-curdling shriek as he flew in through a window. An impressive father earned respect, he knew. But with the cacophony in the ballroom — courtiers screaming, guards shouting, the orchestra attempting something cheerful — only three fainted.

Von Rothbart roosted on the high-backed chair at the lead table. He shrugged off a mantle of feathers and seated himself with his legs on the tablecloth and his boots in a dish of poached boar.

"I suppose the venery for your lot would be an inbred of royals."

No one listened.

He considered standing atop the table but his knees ached after every transformation. As did his back. Instead, he pushed his way through the crowd at the far end, where most of the commotion seemed centered.

He did not expect to find a tearful Odile surrounded by a ring of lowered muskets. One guard trembled so. The prince shouted at her. The king pulled at his son's arm.

Von Rothbart raised his arms. The faux trees shook with a sudden wind that topped glasses, felled wigs, and swept the tiles free of silk leaves. "Stop," he shouted. "Stop and hear me!"

All eyes turned to him. He tasted fear as all the muskets pointed at him.

"You there, I command you to return Elster to me." The prince's face had become ruddy with ire. His mouth flecked with spittle.

"Who?"

"No lies, Sorcerer. Choose your words carefully"

The king stepped between them. He looked old. As old as von Rothbart felt. "Let us have civil words."

"Papa — " cried Odile.

"If you have hurt my daughter in any way — "

A cardinal standing nearby smoothed out his sanguine robes. "Your daughter bewitched an innocent tonight."

"She flew away from me," said the prince. "My sweet Elster is out there. At night. All alone."

Von Rothbart looked around him. He could not remember ever being so surrounded by men and women and their expressions of disgust, fear, and hatred left him weak. Weak as an old fool, one who thought he could ingratiate his dear child into their ranks as a cuckoo did with its egg.

Only magpies would care for such shiny trappings, and they were sorrowful birds who envied human speech.

He took a deep breath and held it a moment as the magic began. His lungs hurt as the storm swirled within his body. He winced as a rib cracked. He lost two teeth as the gusts escaped his mouth. The clouds painted on the ceiling became dark and thick and spat lightning and rain down upon the people.

Odile stretched and caught the wind von Rothbart sent her as the crowd fled. He took her out of the palace and into the sky. It pained him to speak so all he asked her was if she was hurt. The tears that froze on her cheeks answered, Yes, Papa.

The Black Swain

"Von Rothbart!"

Odile looked out the window. She had expected the prince. Maybe he'd be waving a sword or a blunderbuss and be standing before a thousand men. But not the king standing by the doors and a regal carriage drawn by snorting stallions. He looked dapper in a wool suit, and she preferred his round fur hat to a crown.

"Von Rothbart, please, I seek an audience with you."

Odile ran down the staircase and then opened the doors.

The king plucked the hat from his head and stepped inside. "Fräulein von Rothbart."

"Your majesty." She remembered to curtsy.

"Your father — "

"Papa is ill. Ever since...well, that night, he's been taken to bed."

"I'm sorry to hear that. Your departure was marvelous. The court has been talking of nothing else for days." The king chuckled. "I'd rather be left alone."

She led him to the rarely used sitting room. The dusty upholstery embarrassed her.

"It's quiet here. Except the birds of course." The king winced. "My apologies."

"Your son — "

"Half-mad they say. Those who have seen him. He's roaming the countryside hoping to find her. A swan by day and the fairest maiden by night." He tugged at his hat, pulling it out of shape. "Only, she's not turning back to a maiden again, is she?"

Odile sat down in her father's chair. She shook her head.

"Unless, child, your father...or you would consent to removing the curse."

"Why should I do that, your majesty?"

The king leaned forward. "When I was courting the queen, her father, a powerful duke, sent me two packages. In one, was an ancient sword. The iron blade dark and scarred. An heirloom of the duke's family that went back generations, used in countless campaigns — every one a victory." The king made a fist. "When I grasped the hilt, leather salted by sweat, I felt I could lead an army."

"And the second package?" Odile asked.

"That one contained a pillow."

"A pillow?"

The king nodded. "Covered with gold brocade and stuffed with goose down." The king laughed. "The messenger delivered as well a note that said I was to bring one, only one, of the packages with me to dinner at the ducal estate."

"A test."

"That is what my father said. My tutors had been soldiers not statesmen. The sword meant strength, courage, to my father. What a king should, no, must possess to keep his lands and people safe. To him the choice was clear."

Odile smiled. Did all fathers enjoy telling stories of their youth?

"I thought to myself, if the answer was so clear then why the test? What had the duke meant by the pillow? Something soft and light, something womanly..."

The notion of a woman being pigeonholed so irritated Odile. Was she any less a woman because she lacked the apparent grace of girls like Elster? She looked down at the breeches she liked to wear, comfortable not only because of the fit but because they had once been worn by her father. Her hands were not smooth but spotted with ink and rubbed with dirt from where she had begun to dig Papa's grave. Their escape had been too taxing. She worried over each breath he struggled to take.

"...meant to rest upon, to lie your head when sleeping. Perhaps choosing the pillow would show my devotion to his daughter, that I would be a loving husband before a valiant king — "

"Does he love her?" Odile asked.

The king stammered, as if unwilling to tear himself from the story.

"Your son. Does he love her?"

"What else would drive a man of privilege to the woods? He's forsaken crown for thorn. Besides, a lost princess? Every peasant within miles has been bringing fowl to the palace hoping for a reward."

"A princess." Odile felt a bitter smile curl the edges of her mouth. Would his Royal Highness be roaming the land if he knew his true love was a seamstress? But then Odile remembered Elster's touch, the softness of her lips, her skin.

Perhaps Elster had been meant to be born a princess. She had read in Papa's books of birds that raid neighboring nests, roll out the eggs and lay their own. Perhaps that happened to girls as well. The poor parent never recognized the greedy chick for what it truly was. The prince might never as well.

If her own, unwanted destiny of doting bride had been usurped, then couldn't she choose her future? Why not take the one denied to her?

"The rings on your fingers."

"Worth a small fortune." He removed thick bands set with rubies and pearls. "A bride price then? I could also introduce you to one of the many eligible members of my court."

Odile took the rings, heavy and warm. "These will do," she said and told the king to follow her.

By candlelight, she took him down to the dank cellar. He seemed a bit unnerved by the empty cage. She pulled out a tray of blackened eggs. Then another. "She's here. They're all here. Take them."

The king lifted one egg. He looked it over then shook it by his ear.

"Look through the holes." She held the candle flame high.

The king peered through one end. "My Lord," he sputtered. The egg tumbled from his grasp and struck the floor, where it shattered like ancient pottery.

"There — There's a tiny man sleeping inside."

"I know." She brushed aside the shards with her bare foot. A sharp edge cut her sole and left a bloody streak on the stones. "Don't worry, you freed him."

She left him the light. "Find the princess's egg. Break all of them, if you want. There might be other princesses among them." She started up the staircase.

"She stepped on his toes a great deal."

"What was that?"

The king ran his hands over the curse eggs. "When I watched them dance, I noticed how often she stepped on my son's toes. One would think her parents were quite remiss in not teaching her the proper steps." He looked up at her with a sad smile. "One would think."

Odile climbed to the top of the tower to her papa's laboratory. Inside its cage, the wappentier screeched from both heads when she entered. Since their return, she had neglected it; Papa had been the only one who dared feed the beast.

Its last golden egg rested on a taxonomy book. She held it in her hands a moment before moving to the shutters and pushing them open. She felt the strong breeze. Wearing another shape, she could ride the air far. Perhaps all the way to the mountains. Or the sea.

The wanderlust, so new and strong, left her trembling. Abandoning a life could be cruel.

Still clutching the egg to her chest, she went down to her papa's bedroom. He had trouble opening his eyes when she touched his forehead. He tried to speak but lacked the strength.

Her thoughts held *rara lingua* with a certainty that surprised her. As she envisioned her lessons, her jaw began to ache. Her mouth tasted like the salt spray of the ocean. She looked down at her arms. Where the albumen dripped white feathers grew.

She called out, the sound hoarse and new and strange, but so fitting coming from the heavy body she wore. As a pelican, she squatted besides Papa's pillow. Her long beak, so heavy and ungainly as she moved her head, rose high. She plunged it down into her own breast, once, twice, until blood began to spill. Drops fell on to Papa's pale lips. As she hopped about the bed, it spattered onto his bared chest.

She forced her eyes to remain open despite the pain, so she could be assured that the color did return to his face, to see the rise and fall of each breath grow higher, stronger.

Red Caps

He raised his hand to her chest but she nudged his fingers away. Her wound had already begun to close on its own.

When she returned to human form, she touched above her breasts and felt the thick line of a scar. No, she decided it must be a badge, a medal like the prince had worn. She wanted it seen.

"Lear would be envious." Papa said in a voice weak but audible, "to have such a pelican daughter."

She laughed and cried a bit as well. She could not voice how his praise made her feel. So after she helped him sit up in bed, she went to his cluttered wardrobe. "I have to leave." She pushed aside garments until she found a curious outfit, a jacket and breeches, all in shades of red.

"Tell me where you're going."

"Tomorrow's lessons are on the road. I'll learn to talk with ibises and challenge monsters."

"Yes, daughter." Papa smiled. "But help me upstairs before you go."

In the tower library, Papa instructed Odile on how to work the heavy mechanism that lowered the wappentier's cage for feeding or recovering the eggs. The wappentier shuddered and its musty smell filled the room.

"When the time comes, search the highest peaks." Papa unlocked the latch with a white quill and swung the door open. The hinges screeched. Or maybe the wappentier cried out.

Her heart trembled inside her ribs and she pulled at her father even as he stepped back.

The wappentier stretched its wings a moment before taking flight. It flew past them — its plumage, which she had always imagined would feel harsh and rough — was gentle like a whisper. The tower shook. Stones fell from the window's sides and ledge as it broke through the wall.

Odile thought she heard screams below. Horses and men.

Her father hugged her then. He felt frail, as if his bones might be hollow, but he held tight a moment. She could not find the words to assure him that she'd return.

Outside the tower, she found the king's carriage wallowed in the moat. The horses still lived, though they struggled to pull the carriage free. After years of a diet of game meat, the wappentier may have more hungered for rarer fare. There was no sign of a driver.

She waded into the water, empty of any swans, she noticed. The carriage door hung ajar. Inside was empty. As she led the horses to land, Odile looked up in the sky and did not see the wappentier. It must no longer be starved. She hoped the king was still down in the cellar smashing eggs.

Red Caps

She looked back at the tower and thought she saw for a moment her father staring down from the ruined window. She told herself there might be another day for books and fathers. Perhaps even swans. Then she stepped up to the driver's seat and took hold of the reins and chose to take the road.

Bittersweet

THE BOYS ORDERED THE GREATEST HOT
drink ever meant for a glass: Vietnamese coffee. The base of ivory condensed
milk. The top of so-brown-it's-black chicory coffee. The boys marveled at the
dichotomy. Only one coffee shop in Philly offered their favorite. Posters and
flyers covered nearly every wall. The latest single from the Red Caps, a remix of
"Hungry Like the Wolf," way overplayed, hung in the air.

Dault watched Jerrod tip his glass, the lip pale from steam. Doughy and pale,
Jerrod didn't like to break margins. He must have been the first kid to color
within the lines. The sort that regretted spooning peanut butter first from the
jar.

"Would you date a gingerbread man?" Dault asked. The distraction afforded
him the chance to plunge a spoon into his own glass and stir.

"Being diabetic..." Jerrod's forehead creased, making him doubly serious.

"I have you anyways." Dault drank for several seconds to earn a murky mustache. Anything to make his boyfriend grin. It worked. "Someone made a cartoon of the fairy tale. Posted it on YouTube." He wiped his lips clean with the
back of his hand.

"That the one with a wolf?"

"Was a fox, not a wolf. Drink your coffee. Would you rather date a wolf or a gingerbread man?" Dault had often wondered what kissing a wolf would be like. Wolves kiss first and ask permission later. Or maybe never even ask permission.

"Are you dumping me so I can date make-believe people?"

Dault didn't dare hesitate to answer. Jerrod had a list of worries, more than any other guy he'd ever dated. Foot falling off had to be at the top, but the way he would dare Dault to break up with him suggested getting dumped was high on the list. Jerrod's hazel eyes flickering on the table top, as if he were suddenly consulting that list, made Dault regret the joke. "No," he said carefully, "just curious."

Jerrod nodded and smiled. "I think a wolf would snore. Well, maybe I'd date the wolf from the little pigs story. The one who goes after Riding Hood's too straight. And didn't the gingerbread kid run away?"

"Yeah, the whole 'Run, run, as fast as you can!' bit. But I think he'd hitchhike these days. Maybe be all skater on a biscotti."

Jerrod's crutches began to slide down the wall, tearing at band flyers printed on jam-red paper. Dault caught them before they clattered. He'd trip over them, like he had when they first met in Mr. Corlen's seventh period history class. Jerrod had looked so guilty that Dault knew he'd say yes when asked out on a date.

"Why'd he run away?" Jerrod finally took a sip. Dault knew he'd never drink the entire glass. He worried about his blood sugar.

"A pair of dykes made him. They wanted a kid — "

"They couldn't adopt?" asked Jerrod.

"I was adopted."

"Liar. You look like your mom."

"She was adopted too. We came as a package."

"I wish I wasn't related to my folks."

Dault knew that any moment Jerrod would spiral down into some serious moping; his boyfriend's home life was the Unmentionable Topic to be avoided at all costs. But lately, Jerrod had been dropping hints, little *mals mots*. That a bad divorce didn't prevent bad genes.

"I'll adopt you." Dault reached out and ruffled Jerrod's thin blond hair.

Jerrod tried to duck out of the way. "You just want to make me forget about tomorrow."

The flight to Indianapolis with his father. Surgery the very next day. If all went well there'd be weeks of physical therapy. If things went bad, there'd be a lot of therapy. Losing a foot meant all sorts of therapy. Dault told himself not to envision Jerrod trapped in a wheelchair.

"I want to see you walk off the plane."

"Hobble. I'll still have the crutches." Jerrod pushed the glass away from him. "I don't want to go."

"I don't want you to go either." But Dault did. He wanted a whole Jerrod, not a partial. He didn't know if he could be with an amputee. That would make him an awful person — only the worst guy in the world would dump his disabled boyfriend, right?

They had slept together a few times, and it had been awkward. Awkward sex because of blood flow and neuropathy; Jerrod couldn't really get hard. So Dault had to lie back and let Jerrod do things to him. It felt selfish and he found himself making tiny jokes to keep from being anxious.

Red Caps

Afterwards had been just as awkward. Dault would drift off and then suddenly wake, terrified he had kicked Jerrod's bad foot. He would feel his muscles cramp against the task of remaining still for hours while Jerrod's feverish body made the bed feel like an oven.

"Perhaps I can run away," Jerrod said.

"As fast as you can?"

Jerrod nodded. "They really need to change the album. Has it been the same song?" He reached for his crutches. Dault noticed how the others in the coffee shop stared at Jerrod as he struggled to his feet. The protective boot looked enormous, like something an astronaut would wear.

"How did it end for the gingerbread boy?"

"You want another lie?" Dault asked.

"Sure."

"Happily ever after. Met a very handsome fritter and they ran off together."

"Just desserts?"

"I should smack you for that."

"A kiss instead." Dault wished he didn't have to ask.

DAULT WANDERED AROUND PHILLY FOR hours, trying not to worry. Summertime should have been trips to the beach, dripping ice cream cones, exploring underneath the pier and making out in the shade. Not moping. The text message Jerrod sent him hours later didn't help. Jerrod's texts were always so perfect. Never an error, never any shorthand. They had once sat through a bad horror movie and texted back and forth and it took Jerrod three times as long to type his messages.

What if the gingerbread boy wasn't a victim? What if he was a lure? Dropped onto people's plates. He'd have folks chasing him, boys chasing him, and he'd run to that witch's house. The one also made of gingerbread. Think I'm wrong?

Dault replied. *Relx every1 likes gbread how was the flight? Dont b worried luv ya. Maybe you should run, run as fast as you can.*

Dault groaned. He tried calling but Jerrod wouldn't pick up.

That night he fell asleep with the open cell phone hot against his pillow.

BY THE END OF THE WEEK, HIS MOTHER hid the cell phone. She dangled the car keys in front of his face and told him to go out, take a long drive, get some sun and not worry why Jerrod had not returned calls, texts or emails in days. She threatened to spend his college savings on liposuction if he didn't listen.

She only gave him back the phone when he reasoned it wasn't safe to be out on the road without one. Cars break down. Curfews get broken. People get lost.

Like his boyfriend. He wondered if Jerrod had gone all cowardly and decided to end the relationship with silence. Or maybe he had decided to be a martyr — yes, Dault could imagine him doing that, deciding that Dault would be better off not dating a cripple. That word made him sick and ashamed.

He escaped to New Hope with its tidy streets filled with tourists and motorcycle gangs. The restaurants either charged nearly twenty dollars a dish or served hamburgers on paper plates. Leather shops and Wiccan stores and stained glass art.

He sat on the steps outside a tattoo parlor and watched the people walk past. He considered getting a bitter tattoo, something like *Bite me*. Or *Eat me*. He ended up smiling, trying to imagine where would be fun to get inked.

Three boys passed by. Their hair was spiked with product, their tank tops glaring white over tanned skin, shorts drooping below thin waistlines. Golden-

brown skin. The last of the three met Dault's stare and actually turned around down the block to smile at him.

Later, he saw them across the street, entering the ice cream parlor. The third boy dawdled in the doorway a while, offered Dault a slight wave to which he couldn't help but smile. That same boy came out with two cones and ran across the street. A Volkswagen almost ran him down.

"Hey, you look sad." The boy had ginger-colored hair below the lighter streaks. He held out one of the cones. "Go on, take it."

Dault couldn't help but have his fingers brush the other boy's while gripping the waffle cone.

The boy sat down beside him without asking. "So are you browsing or buying?"

"What?" The ice cream tasted like a cinnamon stick that nipped the tip of his tongue.

"Just browsing the boys or looking to take one home?"

Dault blushed. "You bought me ice cream, not a ring."

The boy nodded. He had a chipped front tooth and bit at the scoops of ice cream. "Hang with us. Have some fun." Dault felt his cell phone vibrate in the pocket of his cargo shorts. Jerrod's ring tone, "Average Superstar's Radiate."

"See, someone wants you to come with us," said the boy who wore sandals and had painted his toenails jam-red.

He shouldn't ignore the phone. He never had before. But the hot sun made the smell of cinnamon hang in the air about the boy, who bumped against him, and Dault told himself if he answered and it ended up being that painful conversation where Jerrod told him he wouldn't be coming back, at least not to him, then he'd be left broken. Better to pretend the call never happened.

So when the boy offered a hand to help Dault to his feet, he took it and followed him across the street back to the boy's waiting friends. All their names began with R, but Dault told himself not to pay such attention to remember any of them, not least the ginger-haired boy. That would be something like dating.

By the afternoon, the four of them had walked along to the river. Dault worried about getting lost by the trees. The boy held his hand and guided him around birch and cherry until the path had disappeared. So had the others.

"Chase me," said the ginger-haired boy.

"No, I think I better get back." Dault's cell phone had chirped a few times. Jerrod had left a message.

The boy slapped him on the chest. "Bet you can't catch me." Then he started to run through the tree line. Dault watched him strip off his tank top. His heart

raced as if he were the one being chased. I shouldn't, he thought, but already he had begun to follow.

The way was marked with discarded clothes. A sandal. He saw only one. Shorts. He expected underwear, was curious whether it would be boxers or briefs, when a hand grabbed his arm, pulling him to the ground.

The ginger-haired boy rolled atop him and, without asking, kissed him hard. The tongue that worked its way past Dault's lips tasted sweet. He discovered the rest of the boy less so.

ON THE DRIVE BACK HOME TO NEW JERSEY, Dault listened to the voice message. Route 295 seemed deserted. He was hours late. He still smelled the other boy on his skin.

"Dault, he stole it." Jerrod's voice sounded so weak. Either he whispered or he could barely speak. "The gingerbread boy stole my foot." Nothing more. Dault tried replaying it but the message, the voice, had vanished. Maybe he had been so tired he'd pushed the wrong button. He caught himself beginning to swerve onto the shoulder and kicked the brakes. The tires squealed and he almost cracked his skull on the steering wheel. His chest ached from where the seat belt restrained him. He put the car in park and decided that a good cry might be the best thing.

THE PORCH LIGHT REMAINED LIT AT HIS house. When he pushed the key into the lock, the wood around the doorknob cracked like stale pastry. He pushed a finger past sharp slivers and felt splinters bite.

On the bottom step of the hall staircase was the yellow pad where his mother wrote down phone messages.

Jerrod called. Twice. You got lucky. He felt sick that she had guessed right about spending the night with another boy.

In his bedroom, he threw his wallet on the desk. A scrap of paper, the receipt for the ice cream cone, had the third boy's digits scrawled on it. The desktop computer, sleeping, rumbled to life.

New email blinked over the blurred desktop picture of Dault and Jerrod kissing. Blinked over their eyes, his closed, Jerrod's open and wary of the cell phone taking their picture inches away.

Hey, Dault,

Sorry I have been out of touch. I had to have two surgeries in a row and been mostly sleeping. Guess now you can tease me about being a dope fiend. I have to tell you whatever they put in my IV was amazing stuff. No pain whatsoever.

My foot's all wrapped tight. The doctor (he's this cool guy who's worked on the local football team...does that make me an honorary athlete?) said I should be wiggling toes in no time. But no dancing. I don't dance, remember.

Please, please forgive me. My father's only wanted me to rest.

I must have made your mom crazy tonight with calls. She told me you went out. Please, please call me tomorrow. Hearing your sweet voice would make everything better.

Love,
A whole Jerrod

Dault glanced at his cell phone. That creepy message. Had he imagined it? He rubbed his face and wished the whole day had been a hallucination.
He hit Reply.

Jerrod
Glad the surgery went okay. You need to relax and get better. Don't worry about dancing. I promise I won't ask you to dance.

Dault stopped typing out of fear what he'd write next. He thought about hiding behind some lies. Jerrod would never have to know about the gingerboy. Or would the phone ring again with his conscience on the line whispering to him? He didn't want it eating away at him.

I'll see you when you come back home.
D

He might not be the good boyfriend, a seventeen-year-old Prince Charming, but Dault swore he needn't be the villain. He wished though that he was made of sugar and spice and everything nice.

All Smiles

DROWNING FELT LIKE A REAL POSSIBILITY.

The cold rain came down hard, soaking Saul through each layer of clothing: the faded peacoat he'd stolen from Cotre Ranch, the Red Caps t-shirt he'd bought at their Philly concert, the waffle-weave long sleeve, and the boxers and jeans he'd been wearing for too many days and nights. His socks and sneakers were saturated sponges; every step down the shoulder of the highway made him shiver.

Every time Saul heard a car approach, he would turn back into the force of the wind, letting the rain sting his face. He would squint and, if he didn't recognize the car from the Ranch, he'd raise an arm, thumb out for a ride. And the cars swooshed past and he'd walk on.

By nightfall, the air might freeze him. But he'd been on so many forced marches the last few weeks, he imagined his corpse would keep walking.

A car stopped yards ahead of him. The passenger door opened wide. Saul blinked away the water running into his eyes. A dark sedan, sleek, with tinted windows. A New York-state license plate. How he missed the East Coast! The Statue of Liberty beckoned, reminding him of that speech of hers, welcoming the poor and downtrodden.

Red Caps

He ran up to the car. Warm air seeped from the interior. From behind the steering wheel, a dark-haired girl in her early twenties leaned over and patted the passenger seat, now speckled with rainwater. "Need an ark, Noah?"

A giggle came from the backseat as Saul climbed inside. The vent near his face gushed hot air, a forgotten piece of summer trapped within the car. Saul slammed shut the door just as the girl stepped hard on the gas pedal.

He noticed the glove compartment hung open and stuffed with maps, folded wrong so they accordioned, and papers.

"Introductions," she said. Saul noticed she had the most dazzling smile he'd ever seen. Perfect, expressive, expensive. He caught himself staring at her smile a bit too long, which only made her grin wider.

Saul brushed back the wet hair along his head and offered his name.

"I'm Dutch and back there," she said, stabbing behind her shoulder, "is Marley."

Marley leaned forward and offered Saul a smile that matched Dutch's in brilliance and intensity. He also had dark hair, though his was just shy of stubble compared to her longer tresses. Both wore matching white button-up shirts and black slacks. Both had the topmost buttons undone to reveal plenty of smooth skin.

Siblings, Saul was sure. Both good-looking and with the confidence that meant, if they weren't rich, they had once been so.

"What's a night like this doing to a boy like you?" Marley asked, followed by another giggle that belonged to a toddler.

"Running away," Dutch said. "Well, aren't you? Only someone on the run would be hitchhiking in this weather."

Saul nodded. Cotre Ranch might tell parents it was an "outdoor behavioral health care facility," but it was really a gulag to help kids kick their drug habits through hard labor and obstacle courses. Punishment for doing a little herbal and a couple bumps of crystal meth — how else could he entertain himself? His parents hadn't asked him if he'd like to move from Jersey to Iowa.

The motion of the car and the intense heat made him sleepy. As an inmate of the Ranch, he'd been rising at dawn only to collapse on a stiff bunk every night. And even then, sleep wasn't a guarantee: every so often there were random night checks when a "counselor" would try and sneak up on a sleeping kid. If they could do so without waking him, it meant an hour's worth of scrubbing floors. Saul learned fast to wake at the slightest creak.

"You're not axe murderers, are you?" he asked.

Both siblings laughed. Dutch, at least, had a normal laugh. "No, no. Nothing like that."

Saul's right arm itched. He rubbed it through the pea-coat. He was covered in so many bruises and scabs from all the "tough love." His hands were either all blister or callus.

"No hobo bag?" Marley tugged at Saul's wilted collar. "I always loved those cartoon hobos."

"You're traveling light," Dutch said.

Saul felt too tired to shrug. "Nothing to hold me down." Truth was, the goon staff had locked away most of his things after his parents had dropped him off at the Ranch. He wasn't sure if he should be missing things. What did empty pockets say about a guy?

He looked out the window, scratched at the cheap, tinted film with a dirty thumbnail. The thought of freedom was intoxicating. "I could go anywhere," he muttered. His original plan had been to make his way back to Jersey, but that now seemed as empty of promise as knocking at his parents' door. There was nowhere he had to go, which left him troubled. He couldn't imagine himself anywhere in the world, as if the cold rain had washed away his ability to day-dream. When the siblings let him out, all he would do is wait for the next ride. And then the next.

"We've been anywhere." This time Marley's fingers, which felt like icicles, moved to Saul's matted hair. "And everywhere in between."

Saul stiffened. When you're gay, you always wonder about every guy you see. What if Marley were too? But when you're right, it's still a surprise. It had been too long since another guy had even touched him. While being trapped in a bunkhouse filled with teen rough trade might seem like a wet dream come true, actually no one had the energy after the first few days to do more than brag about past lays. And by the third week, a week of digging holes six feet deep, everyone looked and smelled so scroungy and raw that the thought of even approaching a horny straight boy was too damn hazardous.

"Relax. We want to like you," Dutch said. She ran one finger along the front of her teeth, as if checking to make sure they were clean. Saul noticed she didn't wear any fingernail polish or rings, something he'd expect of a rich girl. She needed only her smile.

As Saul scratched at his arm, Marley's cold touch slipped under his collar. "Are you one of those shy boys?"

Saul didn't think shy was the right word for how he felt. Maybe curious or anxious. When a total stranger started stroking the side of your neck, how were you supposed to act?

His right arm more than itched. It felt as if ants had crawled under the skin. Angry ants that tore at the nerves with their mandibles. He tried pushing up the sleeve of the coat, but it wasn't enough. The arm burned as if soaked in acid. He began stripping off the coat and ripping at his sleeve.

The siblings laughed. "So eager," one of them said, but Saul didn't pay attention to which one.

When he finally bared his forearm, the pain ceased immediately. The skin looked so pale compared to the black, cursive Hebrew lettering of his tattoo. He had thought it so clever to get that line referring to *tefillin* inked on his arm. And *you shall bind them as a sign on your hand*. As a boy, he'd often watch his *zeddie*, his grandfather, on Saturday mornings wrap his arm with the phylactery's straps, which filled the room with the smell of leather. *Zeddie* had told him that the small animal-hide box held magic words.

Of course, as he'd planned, his parents were appalled. He remembered his mother crying, "You can't be buried in a Jewish cemetery. You can't go to *shul.*" He thought her reaction was so hypocritical; after *Zeddie* died, they only went to synagogue for the High Holy Days. The only bagels in Iowa must be frozen in the supermarket.

Saul had expected the staff at the Ranch would mock him for the Hebrew, but Phelps, the head counselor, had admired his tattoo, and actually suggested Saul get more ink, so that it would resemble leather bands coiling all the way down to his palm.

Saul looked at the siblings. Dutch had her eyes on the road, but her face had become drawn, the lines of her jaw clenched tight. "His arm," Marley groaned from the backseat.

"I know," Dutch muttered. She glanced at Saul and the look was one of disgust. Instinct made his hand edge toward the door latch, but he realized that she was driving too fast to make rolling out of the car a safe option. It didn't matter. She pressed a button and the locks came down. He heard them echo a while.

"Remind me that you're not axe murderers," he said weakly. He never wanted trouble.

The last few days had been weird at the ranch; the counselors seemed distracted and kept talking in hushed voices. Some of the older boys were on edge, as if too much testosterone malice had built-up in their veins. Saul was sure they planned on a game of Smear the Queer any moment, and decided he had to get out of there as soon as possible.

That night, he feigned sleep in his bunk. His ears strained to pick out the whispers among the many snores. He hid his face under the crook of an arm and watched as some of the boys rose from their bunks. Saul tensed. He told himself there'd be no shame to kick another guy in the balls if he meant to brain you. But the boys didn't even look in his direction as they opened the door (which should have been locked!) and slipped out of the bunkhouse.

He counted to a thousand. Well, he aimed that high, but somewhere after two hundred, he crept to the door. He held a breath and was rewarded when the handle was unlocked. The grounds were dark, except the amber glow seeping from the slotted windows of the large storage shed, off limits to all but the staff.

Saul knew he didn't have time or the luck to afford being curious.

As he passed through the parking lot, he considered letting air out of the tires, but there were too many cars. He crept down to end of the driveway and looked over the metal gate. Tugging at the chain that fed the motor reminded him of all the bike chains he'd broken as a little kid. He hunted around until he found a palm-sized rock, and then smashed the chain off. He tossed the rock over his shoulder, muttered a "Thanks" to the counselors for teaching him to climb anything, and scurried over the rain-slick bars. He didn't stop running until he reached the highway.

"What do you want to do?" she asked. Saul knew she wasn't talking to him.

"I don't know. I'm hungry though. And we were promised food." The last words came out of Marley as a whine.

Dutch nodded.

Saul leaned against the car door. Now alert, though sweating from the furnace-like heat, he didn't know where to look. Staring at the road left him feeling helpless, but eyeballing Dutch might antagonize her, like an angry dog. He risked a glance and realized she wasn't sweating. Not a drop. His own forehead felt slick, feverish. He remembered Phelps mention he would never trust anyone who didn't sweat.

They drove too fast past a road sign for him to read it. "There's a gas station up ahead," she said.

"We need to stop. I can't think when I'm hungry. I need to think about his arm."

Saul wondered if they were some crazy anti-Semitic pair. Just his luck to find the only New Yorkers on vacation who hated Jews. He tried to cover the tattoo with his fingers, but the skin beneath began to ache again until he removed his hand. He didn't understand what the hell was happening.

Dutch barely slowed down to pull into the gas station. She came to a screeching halt in front of a pump. A pregnant woman filling her gas tank nearby gave them a sour look as she covered her stomach with one arm, as if that might keep her safe from injury. "Looks like we need some gas."

"I need a refill." Marley's usual giggle was brief and pained.

Dutch turned to Saul. "You fill the tank. We'll be inside. If you run, we'll kill her."

Saul nodded. The flatness in Dutch's voice was more chilling than the threat. No, not a threat but a promise of murder.

"C'mon, bro," she said and unlocked the doors.

Saul's legs felt hollow as he stepped out of the car. He moved slowly. Marley flipped him the finger under one eye before following after his sister. Saul noticed that neither of them wore shoes and their bare feet were dark with grime.

Saul hissed at the pregnant woman to catch her attention. She ignored him. He stomped his foot, splashing a puddle. Nothing. Then he noticed the white cord around her neck. Damn iPods. Would serve her right if he ran.

But he wouldn't be so easy to kill. He'd discovered something about himself at Cotre Ranch. Through all the hiking with heavy backpacks, the hand-over-hand rope bridge over mud puddles, the old brick wall they had to climb, he might have stumbled but Phelps's goons had made sure he kept going. They would yell at him, insult him, and shove him forward. And he was tougher for it.

The liquid-crystal display on the pump came to life. He lifted the nozzle. He needed a distraction. On the island beside the pump a metal drum served as a trash can. The crumpled fast-food bags, empty soda cans and discarded oil bottles would ignite fast with a little gasoline. He pulled the nozzle's trigger and splashed the top of the trash.

The pregnant woman finished and drove off. Saul turned to see if the siblings could see him through the gas station's glass windows and found himself face-to-face with Dutch. He jumped back. She was sucking on her index finger. The look of excitement on her flushed face dropped when she smelled the gasoline.

She popped the finger from her lips, and then kicked at the drum. The trash spilled out all around the island. Saul silently cursed.

"Inside," she told him and pushed him toward the gas station door.

Marley stood at the back by the refrigerated shelves, juggling cartons of milk. His lips looked ruddy, as if he'd been kissing someone hard. He'd be gorgeous if not for the smirk. It was the sort of smirk that made you want to punch him before kissing him.

The register drawer was open and empty. Maybe they're just thieves, Saul thought. And they're getting off on scaring me. Then he thought he glimpsed a foot sticking out from behind the counter and he felt the scream building within him. A scream at their madness, a scream of shock and fear. But he knew if he let the scream loose he'd be rooted to the spot and never escape. So he swallowed the scream, as he had the aches and pains he'd earned at the Ranch.

Marley tossed to Saul the smallest carton. Heavy cream.

"The Masai drink blood first and then milk." Marley let one carton drop. It smacked the floor and milk spilt all over the stained linoleum. "Ooops, don't cry." He smiled and Saul shivered, frightened and, embarrassed to realize, aroused. There was something powerful about their Cheshire-cat grins.

Saul glanced around him. He stood in the midst of an aisle with chips and snack foods along one side, soda on the other. Six-packs of root beer caught his attention.

Their smiles had some sort of hold over him. He needed to break that hold, break their smiles, and glass bottles were promising. He'd always thought those scenes in the movies when a guy broke a bottle over someone's head looked hilarious. In real life though, it had to be effective.

Marley opened the carton with his bared teeth and drank. Not a drop ran down his shirt despite the greedy gulps. Behind Saul, Dutch laughed.

Saul opened the heavy cream and lifted it as if to drink. With one swift motion he turned around and splashed Dutch full in the face. She stumbled back. When she opened her mouth to call out, Saul had already grabbed the nearest

root beer by the neck and slammed the bottle into her upper jaw. A couple teeth went flying.

He didn't wait for Marley to react. That was the biggest mistake fresh meat made at the Ranch. During a run, they'd look back to see how far of a lead they had and would lose ground. Or they started to trash-talk. So Saul was already climbing up and over the metal shelving like he'd done so many times at the obstacle course. Bags of chips popped and crumpled beneath him as he scrambled and landed on the other side of the aisle.

But his shoes were still wet. Saul skidded on the floor. He pulled down a spinning rack of travel maps to block the way behind him.

All he had to do was it make it outside. He was sure he could lose them in the woods behind the gas station.

His mistake was noticing the surveillance camera by the ceiling. The barrel turned toward Saul, who surprised, hesitated.

From behind, a strong hand grasped his shoulder and pulled him backward. Ice-cold nails stabbed through the fabrics to bite his flesh.

"We've been too kind to you." Marley's fingernails dug deeper into Saul, making him cry out. Marley slipped his other hand beneath Saul's shirts to stroke and scratch his stomach. "We're no better than magpies. Pretty things distract us."

Saul heard Dutch scream, "Kihl im!" though the words were blurred by her ruined mouth. He felt Marley push his cold fingers down the front of his jeans. Marley nuzzled his ear and the stink of curdled milk made Saul gag.

"That mark poisoned your blood, but I'll enjoy — "

Saul suddenly sprang backwards, slamming Marley into the ATM. They struggled near the coffee station, but Saul couldn't reach one of the hot pots. His fingers closed around the handle of one yellowed, ceramic mug stacked in a pyramid on the counter. Its fellows tumbled noisily to the floor. He slammed the mug into Marley's side and gut. The guy went down, clutching his abdomen.

Saul glanced at the mug, dusty and cracked, a relic older than him. Black lettering on the side said: *Iowa, you make me smile.* He threw the mug at Marley's crotch and ran.

Before he reached the door, his peripheral vision spotted the mop, its wormy head tangled and dripping, before it struck his chest. He stumbled into a shelf, the metal raking his back, cans and cellophane-wrapped goods spilling around him. Dutch shrieked as she slammed the mop against his knees and sent him to the floor.

She stood over him with a slack jaw filled with broken teeth. But no blood; delicate strands of saliva webbed her lips and hung from her chin. She reversed the mop in her hands, so the blunt end hovered over his neck. Saul could see her struggle with her lips to make a smile.

Fresh light played over Dutch. When she raised her head to look out the glass panels, Saul grabbed at her leg, pulling hard. She lost her balance and fell, her head making a sickening smack as it struck the linoleum.

That should take her out, he thought, but she was lashing out, trying to stab at him with the mop. He grabbed the nearest can rolling on the floor — an aerosol, some sort of air freshener — and sprayed her full in the face. She cried out, tried to wipe her eyes as the smell of sweet, faux lemons filled the air.

Saul stood. A car had pulled askew of the pumps and its headlights were aimed directly at the convenience store.

He stopped at the counter — without any urge to peer over and see the body — to grab a lighter. The other stunt from the movies he'd always wanted to try was igniting an aerosol spray.

Outside, the rain had slowed to a steady drizzle. He could still smell the gas vapors from the spilled trash drum.

The driver's side door of the idling car — no, a pickup truck, he saw — opened, flashing Saul the Cotre Ranch "endless trail" logo. Phelps stepped out.

He must have been searching the highway for me, Saul thought. He felt relief at being found. He was more battered and bloody from fending off homicidal siblings than anything the Ranch had thrown at him. And yet, beneath that relief was a dismal emptiness at knowing he'd be brought back to the Ranch. So much for finding a new life.

"Saul, get in the truck." Phelps said, then reached across the truck's seat for something.

Saul stepped into the headlights' beam. "Two psychopaths are in there." He held aloft the aerosol. Despite the drizzle, striking the lighter would probably ignite the very air around him, but he couldn't let Phelps get hurt because of him.

"I know," Phelps said.

"Wait. You...you know?"

"Course." Phelps hefted what could only be a crossbow. "Boys watching the closed-circuit told me you did good." He began walking toward the store.

"But — "

Phelps carefully pushed open the door. "Shit, looks like I'm clean-up crew tonight." He spat on the ground and chuckled. "Get into the pickup. And don't be messing up my radio stations. They're a bitch to program."

Saul noticed that Phelps had left the keys in ignition. He told himself to count to a hundred while the man made the fatalities. If he wasn't back by then...

But he was, with a grin, before Saul reached sixty-eight.

As Phelps smoked a cigarette and drove, Saul had to listen to Patsy Cline walk after midnight and Merle Haggard avoiding mirrors.

"You weren't supposed to even know about their kind till Christmas." Phelps flicked hot ash out the open window.

"Hanukkah."

"Right. Hanukkah." Phelps managed not to mangle the word.

"So the other boys at the Ranch..."

"Some know. We'd been luring that pair through the Internet for months. The boys were supposed to go out hunting tonight. 'Cept someone messed with the gate."

"Guess I'm in trouble."

Phelps didn't say anything but kept driving. The truck's cab was bitter cold from the wind.

Phelps braked the truck to a stop in the middle of the road. "Minnesota is a couple miles north. Just follow the road. Truckstop not far over the border." He pulled out a scuffed leather wallet. "Bounty on two of 'em, let's say two hundred." He held out four wrinkled fifty-dollar bills to Saul.

"I don't understand," Saul said.

"You're the one that ran. Thought you wanted out."

"But —"

Red Caps

"The boys that know..." Phelps crushed his cigarette into a crowded ashtray. "Well, they work extra hard 'fore they can go out hunting. What you went through before, that'll seem like a Hawaiian vacation."

Saul still had the aerosol can in his lap. He could never look at it the same way anymore. Tonight had transformed it from a cheap, lemon-scented air freshener into an aluminum trophy. And he could feel transformed, too. He didn't want to step out of the truck and keep walking down a highway. Not after what he'd seen, what he'd done. He looked Phelps in the eyes. He knew the man was ready to pass judgment, depending on what Saul did next.

He fingered the top of the aerosol. "Ever light the spray? I mean, when you're fighting one of them. Like a mini-flame thrower?"

Phelps slipped the money back into his wallet, back into his slacks. "Never wanted to burn my face off," he said.

Saul knew he had passed the test. They'd turn around, head back to the Ranch. And whatever grueling crap he'd face when he woke would be fine, because this time he'd been the one who chose the Ranch, and this time as reward not some punishment.

Still, he couldn't resist leaning out the window as Phelps put the truck in gear. His hand was steady as he held lighter to the can and squeezed. Saul found himself grinning as a tongue of blue and yellow flames licked the cold night air.

Persimmon, Teeth, and Boys

THE FIGHT HAPPENED ON THE SECOND floor of C-Wing, the science wing. Cecil was climbing the stairs to get to Physics when other kids started to rush past him, pushing his slight sophomore frame back and forth between painted cinderblock wall and metal banister as they calling out that there was a fight upstairs. The promise of violence at high school spreads faster than any rumor or video message, Cecil thought. He knew, of course, who was involved: Bergen Gold versus Robbie Delaski. An image of a mime being stomped by a Tyrannosaurus, the school mascot, came to mind. Then a second image: the dinosaur belching out a bloody, black beret.

A clot of eager, clamoring students choked the far end of the hallway. Cecil was thankful for all their yells; he didn't want to hear Bergen being beaten to a pulp. Still, feeling guilty that he was in some way responsible, or perhaps negligent might be more apt. He tried to press his way through the mob even as teachers came running.

He emerged at the mob's center to see Bergen, his thick nose bent and bloody, lying on the linoleum and staring up at Robbie, whose face looked far worse: dripping red from rutted forehead to chin. Cecil stood amazed that Bergen could have inflicted such a wound — okay, maybe he came to school all sociopath and brought a knife. According to those forensic cable-television shows, scalp cuts were supposed to bleed a lot. Then Cecil saw the paint can on the ground near where Bergen lay. A puddle leaked from the open lid. Persimmon. Poor Bergen. Even when he chose a color as a weapon, he still picked one with a gay name.

Just as the teachers penetrated the inner circle, Robbie's foot slammed into Bergen's jaw. The surrounding kids went silent. Or maybe Cecil stopped hearing their roars. Spittle and blood and teeth erupted, but the only sound was the awful thud of the strike. Bergen didn't whimper, not even as he tried to crawl away while the adults grabbed Robbie.

Cecil watched Bergen helped to his feet and off to the nurse's office. The vacuum where the boys had fought, where the paint and blood spilt, was disturbed as the class bell rang. He spotted a tooth on the dirty tiles. Off-white, broken, tipped crimson. Before someone kicked it away, he'd snagged it. A sharp end bit into the soft pad of his thumb. Bergen's blood mixed with his own. And Cecil found himself late to class because he began thinking of that hokey notion of blood brothers, the stuff of tree forts, frosted cereal, and 1950s television. Eventually, he put the tooth in his pocket, next to his iPod, and went to here all about Bell's inequality.

ON THE BUS RIDE BACK HOME, CECIL found himself scribbling on the front of his physics notebook. But he didn't realize he was doodling until after he'd sketched out a lune, a penny, and a molar. He looked down at the ballpoint drawings as if they were hieroglyphics, not rough sketches. No, worse than hieroglyphics. Alien script. Because Cecil knew he didn't doodle. Not when bored, not whenever. He didn't like art, which seemed to work against math — despite what creaky Mrs. Felisky promised when she handed him a paintbrush.

Now, after today, he really hated art, but it had started the fight forty-eight hours earlier: As part of the School Beautification Drive of '13, all the upstairs halls were to feature student artwork. Mrs. Felisky envisioned Lemane High's C-Wing painted with the faces of famous scientists. Mr. Sedgewick, infamous for torturing every student, favored or hated, by opening the classroom windows during any physics test so that a kid either shivered or sweated, was against such décor. But Mrs. Felisky was more liked than any other teacher at school — little surprise as no one ever secured less than a B- in her courses — so art was going up on the walls.

After class, Mr. Sedgewick questioned why Cecil had volunteered to help — with his grades, Cecil didn't need the extra credit that was the only way to entice the many hands needed to finish the work in two weekends. Cecil shrugged and muttered something about keeping busy to fend off boredom. There were some curiosities he couldn't, he wouldn't express to a science teacher.

Such as his curiosity about Bergen.

Besides being the most talented freshman at Lemane, Bergen was known for being the sole out boy. Ever since freshmen year, he had accentuated a slender build with tight jeans normally worn by girls. He dyed his sneakers while the other cool kids worried over how to keep them bleach white. He moussed his hair into a new shape every week. Even wore a wig or two on occasion. Most of

Red Caps

the students either were baffled by him or laughed at him. Since September had Cecil considered himself among the former. Robbie Depaski was the leader of the other camp.

It was Bergen who devised the clever idea to paint the scientists as they had looked in their younger days — "I'm tired of seeing Mark Twain Einstein," he said with a dismissive wave of his hand. "I want Albie when he was a hot boychik on the prowl for some E equals MC laid."

Tamara Washington tittered. Cecil had trouble deciding where to look: at Bergen, who was pale and wispy, or Tamara's chest which was the opposite but just as bouncy.

Mr. Sedgewick, who had stayed late grading papers, stepped out into the hall. "These murals are about respect, Mr. Gold. The students' choices will be vetted by the science teachers before they grace our walls. I don't want Timothy Leary smiling down at me."

So they agreed to poll the various science classes. The results were the usual boring bunch. Cecil vetoed George Washington Carver — why were the other black kids always stuck on him?—and picked St. Elmo Brady because he had the most awesome name, was really good-looking, and had a Ph.D. Cecil admired all of those attributes.

Bergen insisted on choosing a scientist also. Or else he wouldn't help. Leonardo da Vinci.

"The painter?" asked Tamara. "As in the Mona girl?"

Bergen sighed. "He invented all sorts of things. And he liked men."

"Then why didn't he paint the Mona Larry?" Tamara lifted her hand to Cecil for a high-five. He looked at her like she had prions on the brain. Her hand drifted down. "So what, you have a photograph of young da Vinci?"

Bergen bit his lip. Cecil noticed Bergen wore lipgloss. He wondered what flavor. Did boys who wore lipgloss choose different flavors than girls? Maybe there weren't masculine flavors — Bergen would probably roll his eyes at ever being called masculine — but Cecil was curious. Very curious.

"No. I've only seen his self-portraits when he was an old man."

"Guess you'll have to imagine him young." Molly smirked. "Guess you'll be needin' to go to the men's room for that."

"Oh, where's my diamond ring?" Bergen cupped his mouth a moment and then raised his middle finger to Molly. "Here it is."

"Pisshap. Like some boy is ever going to give you carats," she muttered.

Cecil should never have gone searching the 'net for a younger da Vinci. He couldn't explain why he did it. There was some urge to impress Bergen. To make him grateful. But the consequences of that muddled in the stricter corners of

Cecil's imagination. He wanted to know what flavor lipgloss Bergen wore to make his mouth reflect fluorescent lights so well.

After school, he had found Bergen alone in C-Wing sketching faces on the wall.

"What's this?" Bergen asked when Cecil handed him the color print out.

"I think it's called a palimpsest. Da Vinci must have erased an earlier self-portrait from the page — vellum, that's sheepskin — and written over it. I mean, over the blank. So now, using tech, they've reconstructed what he looked like. I mean, what he drew. Of himself."

Bergen smiled. Yes, his lips did shine pink as a peach, pink as a conch shell. "For me?"

Cecil felt his face grow warm. "Uhh, for the wall."

"Of course." Bergen leaned close. "Since there's the tiniest chance someone might come along, I won't hug you," he whispered.

But then the entire school discovered in the morning that Robbie Depaski, a bully who lacked senior status due to being held back once, and had more hair than a junior should on his face, had spray-painted *F A G* over Bergen's finished youthful da Vinci. He refused to brag about it, or even take the credit, even after he was escorted to the principal's office, but the way he laughed made it clear to everyone that he wasn't the least bit sorry.

And later that day, Cecil found himself shocked by Bergen's revenge with the paint and the resulting brawl. Robbie was given detention for a week. Bergen was suspended from school for three days — but then, Bergen was also in the hospital for observation.

CECIL WAS IN HIS ROOM, READY TO DO HIS

homework at his desk, when he found Bergen's lost tooth in his shirt pocket. He went to the bathroom and washed it clean. The cut on his thumb throbbed and bled fresh. He added antibiotic ointment and an oversized bandage.

Again, he found himself acting weird, his thoughts drifting off to nothing in the midst of an Algebra II problem. When he looked down at the page, the x's and y's and z's had been erased — he could see faint impressions of where they had been written — and poor renditions of mouths with broken smiles covered the page. A plop heralded a red dot on one set of lips. Blood had oozed through the gauze around his thumb and dropped onto the notebook. Cecil rushed the thumb into his mouth, and then remembered when he was a kid, his mother had to put some nasty-tasting medicine onto both thumbs to keep him from sucking them while he slept. The combination of blood, cotton, and ointment sickened him.

He went into the bathroom, not sure if he was going to throw up or not. He had to be sick. That explained everything. He looked at himself in the mirror. Other than wide eyes behind his glasses, he looked the same. He tried smiling to earn a comforting reflection. The grin, toothy, looked fake, like the expression in every school picture taken since elementary school. Then he vomited in the sink.

His mother insisted he drink chicken broth and eat some crackers. He tried for chocolate ice cream, but received a glare from both his parents: No. In bed early — at eight p.m., he felt ten, not sixteen — troubled by homework not even half done, he tossed and turned, unable to get comfortable. His hand went underneath the pillow and grazed something sharp. He sat up in bed, lifted the pillow and saw Bergen's tooth lying on the mattress. He had no memory of putting it there.

The nightlight clicked on, transforming the bland ceiling into a canopy of pale, yellow stars surrounding a fat crescent moon. Cecil rose, gawking at the display. He'd forgotten how his mother would turn the nightlight on before bedtime; he'd been so little then and afraid of the dark. Then he remembered that after he turned twelve he'd asked his mother to throw away the nightlight. He was too old for such things. She had given it to one of her coworkers who had a newborn.

"Very nice, very nice," said a silken voice.

Cecil fell off the bed. When he stood up he saw a man sitting on top of his desk. His skin was darker than cousin Chuck's, and he wore a dove-gray tuxedo but lacked shoes and socks.

> "'Twas a horny night for Mister Moon
> when he saw a youth with a balloon.
> The boy gave a cry,
> his toy reached the sky.
> What a shame they both popped way too soon."

Cecil should have been shocked. Scared. Something. But all he felt was an odd calmness, so he just said, "Hello."

The man raised a hand to his temple in salute. Then he slipped off the desk. "I'm afraid that with the recession all I can offer is a dollar." He reached into his cummerbund and pulled out one of those golden Sacagawea coins. He flipped it up in the air where it glittered and drifted down onto his palm rather than fall-

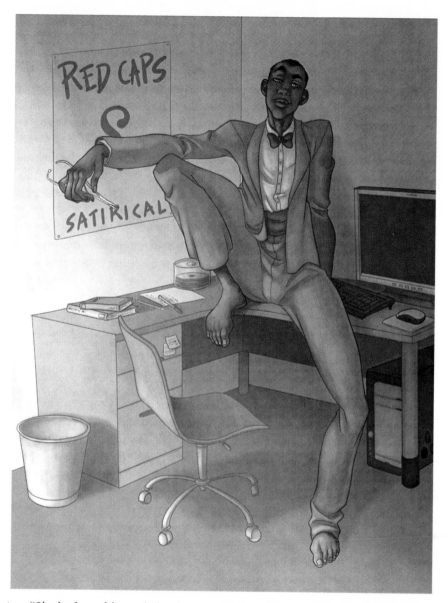

ing. "She had terrible teeth, by the way. Clark and Lewis wagered a dollar — "the coin turned to tarnished silver" — as to whether she'd loose her top incisors or bottom first." The man chuckled. "When haven't men argued over tops and bottoms?"

Cecil nodded though he didn't understand.

"Of course, of more value than a dollar — and let's face it, what would this really buy you anyway? — is wisdom." The man tapped his chin a moment and began walking around Cecil.

"I'm a straight-A student," Cecil said.

Red Caps

"Perhaps you should be giving me advice? Listen to the wise but speak to the fool, I always say." The man's teeth gleamed like washed pearls.

Cecil looked back at the bed. He saw himself lying there, twisted in the covers, mouth open. For a moment, he thought, I'm dead. Then Cecil-in-bed turned. "I'm dreaming," Cecil said and Cecil-in-bed echoed the words with his lips and sleepy breath.

"Of course," the man said. "No one awake ever sees me. That would be dreadful. Just dreadful."

"You're the — "

The man produced a business card from his cummerbund. It featured a black mouse with a gray old-fashioned nightcap atop his head and a pair of pliers in his paws. No words.

"You have to — " the man gestured, rolling his fingers" — you have to turn the card over."

Cecil found the other side read, *Not this side!*

"Over, over."

He flipped once more. The drawing of the mouse had been replaced. *Mr. Bistre S. Ouris. Tooth Sprite.*

Mr. Ouris tsk-tsked. "I know, I know. Not that Cecil is any more...contemporary than Bistre." The way he said it, the name rhymed with *mystery.*

"Tooth sprite." Cecil snapped his fingers. "So that's why you offered money."

Mr. Ouris nodded." Which you so graciously refused. My retirement thanks you." He slapped his hands together and rubbed them, which made a whispering sound. "So, what are you going to teach me tonight?"

"Tonight?"

"I am here, aren't I?" Mr. Ouris folded his arms, but only for a moment. It seemed impossible for the sprite to remain still.

"Me? Teach you?"

"Well you offered. Boasted even about your studies."

"I guess — "

"Ah, ah, ah, first things first." And Mr. Ouris stepped over to the Cecil-in-bed. He reached into his tuxedo jacket and pulled out a wicked pair of needle-nose pliers with mother-of-pearl handles. He snapped the jaws once, twice. "Must get what I came for."

Cecil called out, telling himself to wake up as Mr. Ouris leaned down with the pliers, but Cecil-in-bed just muttered and snored like the last dodo must have before the dogs tore it apart. The pliers hesitated above Cecil-in-bed's parted lips and then, the hand behind them moved fast, slipping the pliers beneath the pillow and out again. The silvery jaws clutched Bergen's tooth.

"Ahh, this one's a fighter. Either biters or fighters." He lifted a loupe from the cummerbund and started examining the tooth. "Hold on, hold on." He glanced down at Cecil. Back at the tooth. Then back at Cecil. He frowned. "This isn't yours...." By the circling starlight it looked like Mr. Ouris had grown a foot taller.

Cecil's eyes widened. "I can explain — " He lifted up his hands, pointing to the tooth.

Mr. Ouris gasped. "I knew it. Knew it. You're a thief. Cunning little hugger-mugger. Well, you won't get a dime off me. I'm broke. Utterly broke."

Cecil backed up against the wall against his poster of the Periodic Table of Accidents between Bi (Blue ice falling from plane passing overhead) and St (Cooking s'mores in toaster).

Mr. Ouris laughed. "Relax, my friend. I'm only licensed for milk teeth. Permanent ones are taboo. Oh, so tempting, but taboo, true black-market trade." He said the last in a mock whisper as he slipped the tooth into his cummerbund. "Well, I must be off. I could say it's been a pleasure, but that will probably be what you dream of after I'm gone." He winked.

"Wait. You don't owe me anything — "

"Damn right," Mr. Ouris said.

" — but you should at least leave something under Bergen's pillow. I mean, the boy whose tooth that is."

Mr. Ouris sighed and bent his head. "Fine." He practically spat the word out of his mouth like it was poison. He then went to the window. He paused, looking back at Cecil. "You know we'll have to break this."

"Why?"

"I must have words with the Superintendent of All Schools. What are they teaching you?"

Mr. Ouris tapped the glass with his pliers. "The quickest way to get inside any hospital is by breaking something. Tibula. Fibula. Nibula." He struck the glass pane, which shattered outwards.

Cecil could see that what lay beyond the jagged edges wasn't ten or so feet off the ground but a white-walled, white-floored hallway. "Hospital?"

"That's where you told me the boy can be found."

The hospital seemed deserted. They passed an empty nurses' station. All the doors in the hall were closed. All but one. Bergen's room.

He looked so small under the white covers. His face looked both less and more striking thanks to bruises. Flowers and cards were on a bedside table along with a pastel water glass, which Mr. Ouris opened, sniffed, then put down with a frown.

"Water." The word came out with disgust. "When did the world turn against high-fructose corn syrup? Oh, sorry day." He sat down in the chair across from the bed, placed his elbows on the edge of the mattress and his long chin on said elbows. "So you like this boy."

"A little. I think."

Bergen snored then, which brought a smile to both their lips.

Mr. Ouris whistled a jaunty tune. "Ahh, young gay love. It's a thing of beauty. Like caries."

"Don't call me gay."

"Ahh, young gay love in denial — "

Cecil shook his head. "I'm not gay."

The sprite rolled his eyes. "And I'm no fairy."

"Label chatter, that's all that is. I hate being labeled. I don't call myself Cecil the Black Kid. Or Cecil the Nerd. I'm an individual. Don't classify me like I'm something found on a museum shelf."

Mr. Ouris tugged at his lapels. "What's wrong with some class?"

"No. Not funny." Cecil looked down at Bergen. "It's not fair."

"Fair? Why should anything be fair?" Mr. Ouris took off his hat and twirled it around one finger. "What do you want, Cecil? Or am I not allowed to ask that because it would be too...labeling?"

"I want..." Too many answers, to many fantasies choked him. Bergen up and whole and smiling, hopefully at him. For the fight never to have taken place. For the fight to have happened and Bergen to have beaten Robbie. For some measure of fairness. Or justice. But that sounded like a bad movie. What slipped out of his mouth was a single word that pushed its way past the other idle thoughts, much as he had through the crowd surrounding the fallen Bergen: "Punishment."

The syllables left a sick taste in his mouth. Coppery. As if he had lost a tooth. He realized he hadn't helped in the fight, just picked up a scrap. His thumb ached and he saw it had dripped blood on the clean, sterile-looking bed sheets.

"An eye for an eye, a tooth for a tooth?"

Cecil nodded.

Mr. Ouris slipped a very tarnished penny out of the slot of his cummerbund and tucked it under Bergen's pillow without even disturbing his sleep. "Some would call those evil thoughts."

"Maybe there's no good or evil, either. Why aren't they as much labels as *gay* and *straight*. There's no absolutes in the world."

"So I'm not a good fairy?"

"You're no angel. They don't exist. You should have free will to do what you want, and the consequences...well, that's what makes someone good." And I did nothing good, Cecil thought. Nothing to help Bergen.

"But doing something wrong wouldn't make me evil, since that's just as much another label, another easy way to classify me, make me easier to understand. There are no tooth spites, eh?"

"Everyone does something wrong in a day. Sometimes more than once in a day..."

"Hmm. Thanks, my friend, I think you did teach me something after all."

Then Cecil woke. He felt warm, stifled by all the covers. He had an embarrassing erection that distracted him for several moments before he searched for Bergen's tooth. He did not find it under his pillow. Or on his desk. He would never find it again.

BERGEN NEVER RETURNED TO LEMANE

High. For several days after the fight, students gossiped: his strict parents sent him upstate to therapy and "cure" him; he ran off to San Francisco and was a street artist; he was afraid. All of them said he was too afraid to return.

Robbie prowled the halls with a fresh-kill smile. His ranking in the cruel hierarchy of high school had improved.

Cecil had stopped doodling. Now and then he would pause in front of where Bergen's portrait of Leonardo da Vinci had been; now the same dun-colored paint used on most of C-Wing's walls covered up the space between St. Elmo Brady and Albert Einstein. Every time he dawdled and stared at the gap, he felt ugly, like looking into the mirror, smiling and seeing one of his front teeth missing.

In study hall the next day, Robbie Depaski screamed as he lifted his head from the table. He'd been napping, his leg a-twitch like a dreaming mastiff's, and now he was clutching his mouth and shrieking. Blood poured everywhere. Spilling through his fingers to stain the front of his football letter jacket. Spotting the table, the linoleum.

The janitor never found any of Robbie's teeth. They closed the cafeteria for the rest of the day.

That night, Cecil's profile on Facebook received a message from Bergen: *When I was in the hospital I dreamt that you came to visit. You brought me a black mouse. I hope that doesn't sound...I don't know, all racist.*

Cecil read the message again and again — he took comfort that Bergen hadn't disappeared entirely, but truthfully he had forgotten his dream of Mr. Ouris until Bergen reminded him.

He typed several possible replies. None were great. They rambled, asked too many questions. He didn't even know if Bergen expected or wanted a reply.

What Cecil settled on was the least pathetic, the least revealing, but he was tired and frustrated and just wanted to click *Reply*. *School seems more intolerable without you. Perhaps I could visit you for real later this week?*

The night passed like water dripping from a faucet — cold and slow and impossible to ignore or sleep away. He would get out of bed every so often and check for another message. Nothing.

A SUBSTITUTE TEACHER MANNED MR.

Sedgewick's physics class. He didn't seem to know why the teacher who rarely ever was absent had called in sick. The DVD player and television were rolled out to the front of the classroom and an episode of *Nova* played. In the dark, many students whispered, goofed off, and one worried. That one was Cecil, who was sure that he had seen a bloody molar on the whiteboard pen tray as he had walked into class. But when he left, there was nothing there other than red stains that could have been left by a leaking marker. Maybe.

Cecil's mood lightened when he saw the reply from Bergen in his message box. *That would be cool with a cap Q.* Seven digits followed.

Why did the act of entering this boy's number into his iPhone seem more momentous than when Cecil asked Jackie Mosley for a kiss in seventh grade on his first date or getting punched in the stomach the next year for staring at Rigoberto Vasquez's uncircumcised penis in the locker room or watching a Dr. Who marathon while influenza and delirium made Cecil convinced these were some lucky guy's home movies?

MOST OF THE STUDENTS WHO WENT TO

Lemane High had smartphones, shopped at the mall and not a Wal-Mart, didn't lack for braces. Not that the surrounding suburbs were rich, and Cecil's parents didn't drive anything with leather interior, but when one of Lemane's teams visited another school district, especially the ones many miles away, the difference in clothes and mannerism was sobering.

Bergen's home was even more deluxe. Cobble-stoned driveway. Awnings of beaten copper.

Red Caps

"Hey," Bergen said when he answered the doorbell's pleasant chime. He wore a prep-school blazer over a white dress shirt — slightly unbuttoned — and khaki slacks. "Just to warn you, my mother is an ovo-flexitarian, so there's a fifty-percent chance of meatball tonight."

"Okay."

"So, what do you think?" Bergen twirled around once in the foyer.

"Nice house."

"No." Bergen pouted and gestured at his clothes. "The uniform?"

"Oh. Preppy."

Bergen groaned. "Not dashing? I know. Navy blue? Can't they make the blazers in a color you don't dare wear to a funeral?"

"How are you feeling?"

Cecil quickly learned through a non-stop ramble on Bergen's part over dinner that the boy's parents were divorced, his father was in Dubai, his mother was an attorney and liked to use her utensils to accentuate whatever point she was making during dinner — which was with meatballs, thankfully. His mother seemed unfazed by her only son's disclosures. As first the salad fork, then the entree fork stabbed the air as she asked Cecil about himself.

The usual reluctance to reveal things to adults made him pause. "I'm on honor roll." That always seemed a fine way to start. Honor rolls impressed parents. "Sciences and math are what I really like. My mother works for Merck and thinks I have a real shot at going to UNC Chapel Hill." He shrugged to punctuate that his future was too far to seriously conceive and served no other purpose but to relate to adults who obsessed over such things.

"Mother put me in a prep school," Bergen said.

She smiled at her son. "It's safer. No offense, Cecil, but the sort of children who attend public schools have the social skills of Neanderthals."

Cecil wasn't sure if the "No offense" was because he still went to Lemane, was black, or didn't know which fork to use first.

"Do you regret throwing the paint?" Cecil asked. As soon as he said it, he saw by her expression that Bergen's mother did not approve of the question.

"Nope. It was the only time Robbie looked pretty."

She took a sip from her wineglass." The entire situation should never have happened. And we're not allowed to discuss the matter while there's a lawsuit pending."

After dinner, Bergen took Cecil into the den, which could have swallowed a classroom. The flat-screen television would give the whiteboards a run for their money.

"So." Bergen slouched on one of the comfy white sofas.

"Yeah."

"Mom's intense."

"I think it's part of the rules," Cecil said.

How would his own parents react if he brought home a boy? A boy like Bergen? Shocked that Cecil was into guys? Thrilled that if it was a guy he came from money? His parents' mindset was an utter blank to him; they never pressured him to date, never asked him anything embarrassing around Valentine's Day or about school dances. He had learned about pregnancy and adolescence's roller coaster of hormones from a book they had left for him on his bookshelf when he had been a naïve twelve year old and opened wide the flap in the front of his pajama bottoms to his father and asked him about the black wiry hairs around his penis.

His dad had never given him a condom. He had bought him a membership to *Smithsonian* magazine.

"But I think she'd let me date a Neanderthal if I could, you know, My Fair Lady him."

"Huh. What?"

"It's a movie." Bergen laughed. "Oh my gawd, your eyes went so wide."

"Sorry."

"Listen, it's the twenty-first century, so I feel there's this pressing need to just stop all the hints and whiffs."

"Right." Cecil had no idea what Bergen was talking about. He realized that, outside of the hospital, this was the only time he had seen Bergen without lipgloss. The uniform diminished much of his...flamboyance.

"So." Bergen put a hand on Cecil's shoulder. His fingertips pressed, rubbed, stroked a little. "I'm just going to ask you out."

Cecil nodded, even as words tumbled out of his mouth. "So you think I'm gay?"

Bergen rolled his eyes. "I practically have my arm cuddling you and you haven't moved away."

"Yeah." Cecil breathed in deep. "Remember how that word 'faggot' bothered you — "

Bergen slipped his hand off Cecil. "Bothered is a little mild...try offended. And he ruined my — "

"True. All true. I just...I just don't know if I want to be called gay. By anyone."

"It's not as bad as faggot — "

"No. I know. But I wouldn't want you to be introducing me around as your black boyfriend anymore than as your gay boyfriend."

Red Caps

"Everyone would know you're my gay boyfriend since you'd be me with. Or are you bothered because I'm too flaming for you?"

Bergen rose and paced the room a moment, then turned on the television with the remote and began exploring all that Netflix had to offer that day. He didn't look at Cecil when he said, "It's not easy to step out of the closet. I mean, I've known forever. Everyone has to come out their own way. And some of us like to burn bright."

"I love how you express yourself." Cecil stood up and forced himself to walk over to where Bergen stood staring at listing for Musicals. "I think it's amazing you doused Robbie in Persimmon. And you're wittier than anyone I've ever met."

"There's a 'but' coming..."

"I think — I think I was arguing this with someone else. Trying to make him understand. Words like 'gay' and 'faggot' are like name tags we stick on our shirt. Or like when our moms wrote our names in our clothes when we were in kindergarten. You don't have to wear them."

"You're afraid." Bergen turned around. They were close enough to kiss but Cecil knew by Bergen's furrowed brow that was not going to happen. "You're afraid of being called a faggot, too."

"No. I'm scared that I'm going to have to abandon the things I do care about just because I'd date another guy. That I'd only be accepted if I like fashion." He took the remote from Bergen. "Or musicals instead of science-fiction movies. I don't want to change myself to fit a label. I didn't know what Persimmon looked like before I met you. I don't want to have to know all the other colors just so you would feel comfortable with me."

"I-I don't understand. It's not like saying you're gay suddenly turns you into a drag queen."

Cecil hung his head. The sight of their so different shoes in the thick carpet made him think back to the last time he had gone to a quiz bowl at a poorer school. His sneakers were worn around the edges. Dingy. Bergen had shiny loafers. They looked like they had not only been bought at two totally different stores but two different cities. Or even countries.

"Can I — do you have any aspirin. I kinda have a headache..."

"Sure." Bergen looked deflated. Insulted. "I'll go — "

"Just tell me where the bathroom is. I have some, uhh, other business I need to do, too."

Cecil opened the medicine counter. As he had anticipated, the nearest prescription bottle was for Bergen. Vicodin. Under the masking sound of the running tap, he shook out two pills and pocketed them.

When he came out, he took hold of Bergen's arm. "I did want to spend time with you. Can we still watch a movie?"

Bergen gave a weak smile and nodded.

THAT NIGHT, CECIL TOOK BOTH VICODIN.

He waited until he felt dopey, almost waited too long as he began to stumble and had to sit down at his desk and his arms slipped now and then. He had to be precise as he lifted the pair of needle-nose pliers he had found in an old toolbox in the garage. But he didn't want to feel the pain as he clenched the metal pincers around one of his back teeth.

He didn't even remember pulling; it must have been hard work because both the pliers and the tooth flew across the room. He felt warmth fill his mouth and run down his numb lips. He brought up an old shirt to soak up the blood.

The tooth, still gory, was slipped beneath his pillow. He lay half under the covers, brought one arm over his eyes, and counted for as long as he could remember, which was not very long.

WHISPERING IN HIS EAR WOKE HIM. "BRIB-

ery? Oh, my boy, you know me too well."

Cecil opened his eyes. He sat at his desk. Stretched out on his bed, hat tipped to cover his eyes, was Mr. Ouris. He wore animal slippers, fuzzy mice.

Cecil didn't feel the drowsiness of the drugs or the pain of the lost tooth. He tongued the empty spot in his mouth but it didn't set his nerves on fire.

"You must be desperate," Mr. Ouris said. "Or worse, have a conscience. You asked for revenge, and I've been obliging you. Just tonight I removed some rather nicotine-stained teeth from a very loud-mouthed girl you dislike. I'm inundated with incisors, bristling with bicuspids — "

"Stop."

Mr. Ouris raised his hat and frowned. "What? Now? But I've been having so much fun since you taught me I don't need silly trademarks or denominations."

"No. Stop. Talking."

"Someone is snappy." Mr. Ouris chattered his teeth a few seconds, then covered his mouth with one hand, the other gesturing for Cecil to speak.

"I don't even know what I was thinking summoning you. But you're different, you're in this world, you're not, you're the only one that ever seemed to have listened to me — though I'm kinda scared at what has happened from that.

"I just want things to be simple. But they can't be because simplicity demands classifying *everything*. This is gay. This is not. This is a kiss, this is not. There

Red Caps

aren't any in-betweens. People don't want there to be. They need to have everything defined, and I feel like if I do that, instead of finding myself, I'm losing myself altogether."

"My turn?" Mr. Ouris mumbled through his fingers.

Cecil nodded.

"Je suis une souris. Je suis aussi une fée."

"What —"

"My turn, remember. Merci. What I just said are facts. And what I just said is meaningless because you do not understand French. Life and love can be both true and meaningless, alas."

He held up Cecil's pulled molar. "Call this a tooth, a snag, a chopper, a clicker... whatever you like, but it will do what it is meant to. Everyone knows that but we like words as we enjoy play. Referring to this as a bit of ivory might get you a bad grade in English class but it won't make it any less a tooth.

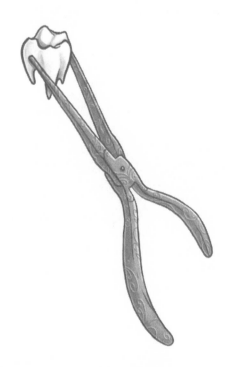

"So you like boys. And you've liked girls in the past, too. You can howl at the moon all you like, but you will be called gay or queer or pédé as much as you will be called black, African-American, maybe even nigger. Again, I say words can be both true and meaningless."

"So then, Bergen was right. I am just scared of being called a faggot."

Mr. Ouris tossed Cecil the tooth. "Perhaps. That's what happened to him, so he thinks it's true and he thinks your fears are meaningless. But perhaps you're right. You're simply a Cecil Gibson. Fact. And all that people will call you in this life is meaningless as long as you stay true to who Cecil Gibson is."

"I don't even know who I am half the time. I asked that girl out years ago. Now I want to be with Bergen — who probably never wants to see me again — and tomorrow, who will I be then?"

"Put the tooth back in."

"Hmm?"

"Stop playing with it and put your tooth back in."

It fit perfectly in the empty socket. Didn't even wiggle loose.

Mr. Ouris appeared over Cecil's shoulder. "I don't think mortals were ever meant to live past fifty. Otherwise you'd have milk teeth and beer teeth and then prune-juice teeth. But your kind does live long these days. Gone are the old rules. I'm not even following them now. I don't know what will happen tomorrow. Maybe I'll be tired of all the grisly effort and stop haunting your school. Maybe I'll go back to plucking the tooth of babes. Or I could try collecting from sharks. I hear they never stop growing teeth. Imagine that. Though they don't sleep do they?"

"Mr. Ouris — "

He waved. "No thank you needed. But as you once said, actions are what define you. If you're willing to tear out one of your own teeth, you're pretty damn brave. And foolish. So, act on your feelings, and whatever others call you, whether it's true or not, treat it as meaningless."

Mr. Ouris slapped Cecil on the back, which knocked the tooth out of his mouth. "I never really planned on giving this up..."

And when Cecil woke, he wished he had saved one of those Vicodins because the pain was terrible. But not enough to stop him from texting Bergen an apology. Or doodling a plan.

GOOGLE FOUND THE IMAGE HE WANTED.

Software added a sepia tone. Staples turned it into a poster that would stick to any wall. And so, before going to lunch, Cecil went to C-Wing and the blank patch among the scientists' portraits. He slipped the cardboard tube out of his

Red Caps

backpack and stretched high on his toes to ensure that a young da Vinci returned to where he belonged.

And before anyone could take it down or stain it, he took a photo with his phone and sent it to Bergen, who moments later replied with a toothy-grin emoticon.

Gomorrahs of the Deep,

a Musical Coming Someday to Off-Broadway

WHEN I WAS SEVEN, MY BABYSITTER SAT ME down on the plump couch in our basement and promised me an entire bowl of butter-pecan ice cream if I would be quiet while she watched a DVD. I think she had a report due for class and had decided to rent the movie rather than read the book. As the opening credits ran for *Kiss Me, Kate* I stuffed spoonful after spoonful into my mouth. But by the time the cast sang "We Open in Venice" I had forgotten about the ice cream and stared wide-mouthed at the television. My legs began to swing with the music, upsetting the bowl. Melted, sticky goo spilled over both our laps.

That night my eyes opened to new wonders, my ears heard a new heartbeat. I began begging my parents to buy me that DVD, and others, too. My fairy tales were movies featuring Princes Charming like Danny Kaye and Gene Kelly. I didn't lack for ogres — such as Audrey II from *Little Shop of Horrors* — or wicked witches with appetites — for that, there was Lola from *Damn Yankees*.

Since then I have wished life were more like musicals. But people don't burst into song and dance when their emotions rise or fall. Mouthing lyrics while listening to your iPod or wailing in the shower while shampooing your hair don't count. I want a chorus to warn me of danger while singing verse. I want the romance of being serenaded, of the duet. And all I get is high school.

ONE NIGHT, MY BOYFRIEND ASKED ME TO

come over to study. My hope was we'd be making out rather than struggling through *Moby Dick*, a book that squashed my brain like a lead weight whenever I tried to read more than a few pages. Then I saw what Hugh had done to his bedroom. Photocopies of thick-bearded old men had replaced the posters of Bob Dylan, Morrissey and the Red Caps.

"Herman Melville and Walt Whitman," he said, with the blatant ardor most gay boys reserve for pop stars thick with eye shadow or young actors infamous for stripping off their shirts on film.

"Like the bridge?" My experience with Whitman involved crossing the Delaware River from South Jersey into Philly so we could hit the Trocadero Theatre to watch indie bands.

"Like *the* gay poet."

"Oh." I collapsed on his messy bed. I lay on my stomach and rested my chin on my hands. "So you like...really want to study?"

He nodded. "Remember, our oral presentations are due this week."

"Fine," I sighed. Being at the tail end of the alphabet, I had planned on procrastinating until Thursday. "Can we work out an incentive program? I'm thinking it's about time someone invented Strip Book Report."

Hugh raised an eyebrow, the left, with its errant hairs. I wanted to pluck it to a fine curved arc while he slept. But it matches his mop of unruly curls. "Not book reports...oral presentations — "

"Imagine. We take off our sneaks after writing the introductory sentence." I rolled over and dramatically kicked off one cherished Converse All Star. "State our thesis, off come the shirts. By the time we're at the conclusion, the floor is covered with our clothes." I stretched my head back, off the side of the bed, and offered my best leer, seventeen years in the making.

He leaned over and kissed me. A bit sloppy, but that's fine because we both laughed. Then he shook his head. "No. I need to work on this."

"So I'm moral support. I can help you navigate Wikipedia for answers."

He clamped a hand over my mouth at that. "Heresy!" I stuck my tongue out and licked his palm, which doesn't taste that great but one has to know. No boyfriend is ever perfect.

"I have this *tremendous* idea."

When he took his hand away, I felt the beginning of a frown. Hugh's ideas, especially when he considers them *tremendous* or *monumental*, usually end up being problematic. Like last summer when he decided to rewrite Shakespeare's *Taming of the Shrew* as a webcomic featuring actual critters. I cured him by downloading the awful movie *The Killer Shrews* on my netbook and loudly playing clips whenever he mentioned the otter Petruchio falling for a furry Kate.

"Do tell."

"I'm going to do a whole presentation — not some sixth-grader's book report — on the homoeroticism in *Moby Dick*."

Red Caps

I laughed. Awful move. Worse, I told him: "You might as well sing it."

His expression grew pensive, then hurt. Like last summer when he went through a phase he called Inner Fat and wore nothing but baggy clothes. At one point, I pulled his boxers over his navel without giving him a wedgie and told him he was ridiculous. He sulked for nearly two weeks before I dragged him free of the bad mood by insisting he watch quirky French films with me.

"It's not a dumb idea."

I sat up in his bed. "I never said that. But even if there's some gay in the book — "

"There is. Lots. Whole scenes." He blinked at me, as if trying to wake from a bad dream. "Didn't you read it?"

"I'm more a SparkNotes kinda guy. But why would you want to rub their noses in it?"

"They're not puppies," he said.

I suddenly envisioned the students in Mr. Shimel's English class as dogs. Tracy Borland's thing for scrunchies earned her labradoodle status. Brian Coleman's jaw belonged to an English bulldog. When Derek Fiesler wore his basketball jersey — a glimpse of muscled arm and hairy pits! — that would be one hot Great Dane.

"Besides. I'm out. You're out."

"But neither of us wears pink shirts. We're like...assimilated. Why call so much attention to being different? Different is death in high school."

"I'm tired of acting like everyone else," he said. "We're not — "

"Maybe I am."

"You're not. You're a theater geek."

"I prefer *thespian*."

"You work stage crew."

"Ersatz thespian."

"You just used the word 'ersatz.' That's an SAT expression."

"Now a good vocab is being lavender, too?"

"Help me," he said.

I shook my head. "And feel all those fears from when I first came out rush back into my chest? No thanks." Even as I said that, my heartbeat raced faster, my stomach parkoured around my middle. I didn't even want to be in class if he was going to be writing G-A-Y on the whiteboard in front of everyone. I heard phantom laughter. "Not with this." I grabbed my backpack, zipped up my hoodie and left his room; rushing down the stairs, I didn't even bother to call out a good-bye to his folks.

The suburban streets were quiet and cold, but my anger was keeping me warm. It was late November, but few houses on the block were lit because the neighborhood prefers menorahs to tinsel. I kept to the middle of the street. My hands were tucked away in the pocket of my white hoodie.

I soon heard my boyfriend's car whining behind me. When he rolled down the window, music from the radio filled the air.

Then he sang:

> *Get in the car. It's cold. Don't be so angry all the time.*

I kept walking, but more slowly.

> *Get in the car. Don't make me beg. Don't make me rhyme.*

I stopped and turned.

> *Don't call me Ishmael.*

"I won't." he said. "Your name is Greg."

I took a step forward, resting my hands on the open car window.

> *Tell me you won't go through with this. Tell me that tomorrow will be sane.*

He shook his head.

> *I can't. I won't. Don't you see? That would go against my grain.*
> *They'll laugh at you and, if I stand by you, me as well.*
> *What else does English class do than make our lives a hell?*
> *It's only Melville.*
> *Only Melville?*

I kicked his car door, shouted, and walked away.

> *Don't call me Ishmael!*

He drove after me.

> *You're afraid of what? That I'll make of fool of us?*
> *But I can't stay quiet anymore.*
> *It's just a book about a whale. Nothing else.*
> *You're finding fags where there aren't, all to start some stupid war.*
> *You saw the line. "Bosom friends."*
> *If that's not the gayest thing you ever heard a sailor say —*

I blinked into the glare of his headlights.

> *I'm drawing a line. Right here and now on the street.*
> *Abandon please this Moby Dick essay.*
> *It's only Melville.*

He stopped the car and leaned his head out the window.

> *Only Melville?*
> *Please. Don't call me Ishmael.*

He opened the driver's side door.

> *He had a voice. Like any of us, he wanted to be heard!*

He's long since dead. Are you some literary nerd?
I won't put the man in the closet, like all the teachers do.
He's better off in the dark. Find another book to review.
Why won't you be my Ishmael, why won't you be my first mate?
I need your strength for this effort, I need you to relate.

I stepped back from the car.

I'm not some Ishmael, I am only a Gregory.
You'll do this alone. I won't be part of some classroom...infamy.

And I ran all the way home.

THE NEXT DAY, DURING LUNCH, MY BEST
friend Casey lowered her vintage cat-eye glasses farther down her nose and then poked me with a french fry. "You look like someone took away your pixie sticks and your parents blocked Bravo."

"I had a fight with Hugh."

She dipped the offending fry into mayonnaise puddled atop a napkin on her lunch tray. "Not 'we had a fight.' So you admit this was all your fault?"

"Did not!"

"Well, what weren't you solely guilty of offending him with?"

"He wants to give a presentation in Shimel's class. On how gay Melville was."

"What's wrong with that?"

"It's crazy. Capital-C crazy. The kids will tear him apart."

Casey rolled her eyes. "Please. You know how much of the assigned reading has a gay subtext? We're all used to it by now." She nudged Sharon, who was sitting beside her, causing her to spill milk down her chin. "Right? Some of us like reading about all that boy-smooching."

Casey stood on the bench.

If you squint real hard you'll actually see
great works of literature don't shy from sodomy.

My eyebrows rose. I glanced around but the rest of the cafeteria seemed ignorant that a senior wearing thrift store chic was singing in their midst. They only cared about their greasy carbs or wilted salads.

It's all subtext, I'll have you know,
of boys wanting to find some beau.
Read 'tween the lines if you don't believe me.

Then Sharon and the other girls sitting at our table lifted their lunch trays over their heads, swiveled around and swayed.

And we girls, how we love to think of those guys

stranded on the beach in Lord of the Flies,
waiting for fair-haired Ralph to conquer his Jack,
while the choir boys 'round them didn't hold back.
Casey kicked away a foil-wrapped burger.
Think fan-fic is only recently?
I'd wager folk in the sixteenth century
wanted that hunk Romeo
to dump Juliet for Mercutio.
Read 'tween the lines if you don't believe me.

Red Caps

The chorus of girls joined in:

> *And we girls, how we love our gamecock.*
> *That Watson adored his roomie Sherlock.*
> *Sure Doyle gave the good doctor a wife,*
> *But we all know Holmes was his fantasy life.*

Casey leaned down and offered me a hand to step up onto the table. I shook my head no, so she grabbed my arm and pulled me up with surprising verve.

> *Mark Twain's books aren't immune to such gaiety.*
> *Or did you miss the crossdressin' Huckleberry?*
> *Running off with his Jim*
> *for reasons not so prim.*
> *Read 'tween the lines if you don't believe me.*

"You're crazy," I said. And looked down to see I had stepped in mac 'n' cheese. My poor Converses. Dairy and canvas don't match.

After cleaning off in the bathroom, I was late to algebra. Ms. Benress turned from the blackboard, already marked up with problems galore, to give me the stink-eye as I took my seat.

I began copying x's and y's in my notebook. Why anyone would ever want to add two such different numbers was beyond me. X's were...well, like me. A bit naughty by nature (you never see moonshine jugs with YYY on them or hope to see a Y-rated movie). X's were complicated. Like an intersection or a crossroads. But passionate, especially with O's. But Hugh was totally a Y. Always wondering about things. Y this? Y that? And yet...you couldn't spell so many wonderful words without Y. *Dearly. Sweetly. Smartly. Yummy* needed two.

Ms. Benress asked the class who would like to solve the latest equation she had chalked on to the board. Hands went up. Not mine. Yes, still she called on me. I groaned and slid out from behind my desk.

But my mind wasn't even attempting to do the algebra. Instead, it put words to the patter of my feet, the tapping of someone's pencil, even the ticking of the old clock on the wall.

> *Answers aren't ever easy,*
> *not when you're unsure you're right.*
> *Not when you love him dearly,*
> *perhaps I'm just too uptight?*

"The X's and Y's please," Ms. Benress said.

> *X marks the spot of my heart.*
> *Only one boy has the map.*
> *If singing keeps us apart,*
> *I'll end up feeling like crap.*

How does he ever love me
when I only question Y?
What I've done, what misery.
Who wants to say good-bye?

I dropped the chalk, I turned from the board and headed out the door. I knew that Hugh would be eating lunch and headed back toward the cafeteria.

A hall monitor looked up from his paperback. He held up a hand to stop me.

Please let me make amends now.
I'll risk two days detention,
to tell him my solemn vow.
Please, I need his attention.

The monitor teared up and nodded his assent.

I ran to the cafeteria doors, pushed them open and...

...everyone but Hugh in fifth period lunch stared at me. Not Hugh because he wasn't there.

"Sorry," I muttered.

I waited for him by his locker as the bell rang.

He offered me a weak smile, the sort that is armor for your feelings. I had never hugged him at school before. I wanted to now, right then and there, but hesitated. He opened the locker door between us. More armor.

"You didn't eat lunch?" I asked.

He shook his head. "No, I went to the library to work on my report."

"Maybe I can help?" I rubbed at his shoulder.

"You haven't even read the book."

I winced. "True. Well then, can I borrow your *Dick*?"

"What?"

"The Melville. I want to know what all the fuss is about."

He lightly rapped the back of his head against his locker door. "What happened to your copy? We were assigned the book a month ago — "

"That reminds me to ask Amazon for a refund. Super Save Shipping my ass."

" — and my presentation is today."

"Yes, but it's eighth period, last period of the day. I'll give it back before seventh. Promise."

"Fine." He handed it over.

I made sure to brush his fingers with mine when I took the book from him. He sighed, a sign — I hoped — that he was shedding some armor.

Red Caps

I BROUGHT THE BOOK WITH ME TO GYM

class. Yeah, Mr. Meno yelled at me, demanding I drop it, but I told him that the school board was far more concerned with me exercising my mind than my body. He growled a bit but ignored me for the rest of the class.

I could see that Melville liked his words, but I wasn't so much interested in what he wrote as I was following in the thread of notes that Hugh had made. They led me to one ongoing passage about Ishmael squeezing lumps of whale spermaceti — which I hoped wasn't what I thought it — *ugh* — with other deck-hands. Hugh had written in tiny scrawl around the margins. I thought of secret codes and a thrill went through me:

Clearly this is Melville's attempt to show not only the joys of masturbation but how such an affectionate act can bring men closer.

I grinned and fought down a massive giggle. Hugh had written *masturbation.* Serious Hugh. I wondered if he got turned on while reading the passage, which seemed more gross than erotic to me.

Once the thirty minutes of chin-ups, push-ups and near throw-ups surrounding me were finished, I followed the other boys to the locker room, sat on the scarred wooden bench that ran down the middle of one tunnel of lockers and read more.

Before I had turned more than a couple of pages, though, I noticed that the usual accompanying din of guys changing and showering had...a rhythm?

I looked up from Melville to see a line of seniors, bare-skinned except for the towels wrapped around their waists, heading off to the showers. As they passed each locker, they slapped the metal door with their palms in a steady staccato, which they matched with a chantey:

Yo, all young fellows that just might be queer
for me, way hey, blow the man down.
Best pay some attention and listen here.
Give me some time to blow the man down.

I set the book down on the bench and cautiously stepped to the end of the hall, watching the line of boys as each stripped off his towel and threw it onto a hook — every one landing with perfect precision — before they stepped under hissing shower heads.

I'm a high school senior fresh from Jersey.
Breaking hearts because I have no mercy.

I edged closer. The testosterone in my blood reacting like iron filings to a magnet. As the guys sang, they soaped themselves. The steam from the hot spray obscured...well, all the good parts, like a cartoon censor.

113

Gommorahs of the Deep

When a cute guy is wanting a date
with me, way hey, blow the man down,
when our bodies touch that just might be fate.
Give me some time to blow the man down.

Red Caps

Each slick boy squeezed the soap in his hands — like the sailors of the Pequod had worked the spermaceti — causing the bars to leap into the air, only to be caught by the boy next in line. Not since I was seven had my jaw hung so low.

> *Then tomorrow there'll be another boy*
> *all while yesterday's one sheds tears ahoy.*
> *You want me? Dare you take me home tonight?*
> *For me, way hey, blow the man down*
> *I'll leave your bedside, my exit stage right.*
> *Give me some time to blow the man down.*

I turned away from temptation...after a second look. I grabbed *Moby Dick* to shield the too-obvious effect of the chantey performance on my mainsail.

I ran into Hugh just before he walked inside his seventh-period class.

"Hey," he said.

My response was to tug him hard in the direction of the nearest boys' bathroom; he started to complain, but I told him French class could wait.

Once inside, I shoved him into a stall. I had a lot of enthusiasm to work out of my system.

He met my kisses with guarded measure. "But...I'll be...late."

My lips ate his words up. I slid one hand around to the back of his polo shirt, another hand to the front of his chinos.

He pressed his face into the crook of my neck and gasped. He managed to say, "Not here. Come over tonight. We'll watch *Les Chansons d'amour* again."

My favorite film. "Promise?" We lost our virginity to Honoré's lyrics and Beaupain's score. I squeezed him tight as the echoes of the experience filled my head and chest.

"*Tu doives entendre je t'aime,*" he said softly into my ear.

I stepped back. We chuckled at our obvious erections. His hand cupped my face for several seconds. Then we left the stall and sought to look more presentable.

"This is the greatest book ever," I said.

"Really?"

"No. But this may be the greatest day ever for me."

He kissed me again, on the cheek. "Don't be late for English. I'll need you there to cheer me on."

I decided, then, to skip study hall. I knew I had to do more than just applaud my boyfriend's efforts.

"WHERE DID YOU GET THE GUITAR?" HUGH

asked when he saw me sitting in the front row in English. For the first, and last, time.

"I borrowed it from the music department."

He smiled. "Do you even know how to play?"

"No, that's why I borrowed a guitarist, too." I waved toward Casey, who had cut class for a noble effort. "She owns every one of the Guitar Heroes."

When Mr. Shimel called Hugh to come up to the front of the class and begin his presentation, I followed.

"It's a duet," I told the heavyset teacher.

Hugh cleared his throat.

> *Ships are like prisons, don't you know*
> *men kept with other men on decks below.*
> *Melville knew this from his life at sea,*
> *he found homosexuality.*
> *Let me tell you about the Gomorrahs of the deep.*
> *Let me tell you about the Gomorrahs of the deep.*
> *Proof's in* **Moby Dick,** *his most famous book.*
> *Never were sailors so damn tight. Take a look.*

Tracy Borland giggled, instigating an infection of chuckles and chortles that spread to the students around her. In response, I threaded my fingers between Hugh's to hold his hand tight. Then I pressed against Hugh, as if spooning him (which would happen tonight) as I sang the next verse.

> *Think of that savage islander Queequeg.*
> *In bed he harpooned Ishmael's pant leg.*
> *What about that chapter where they all squeeze*
> *out lumps of whale gunk, isn't that just a tease —*

Brian Coleman's wide mouth stopped masticating a lump of pinkish gum. Hugh smiled.

> *To boys like me, who search each book each day*
> *for characters like me, proud to be gay.*

Derek Fiesler grunted out "No way..." so it was only fair that I winked at him. His face flushed and he looked away.

> *Ships are like prisons don't you know*
> *men kept with other men on decks below.*
> *Melville knew this from his life at sea,*
> *he found homosexuality.*
> *Let me tell you about the Gomorrahs of the deep.*

Red Caps

Let me tell you about the Gomorrahs of the deep.

Melville wed, had a wife, that much is true.
But his real love was Hawthorne, a dude —
yes, that man who gave us The Scarlet Letter —
Melville's heart ached to know much better.

Before you say foul at what we have found
step wise and meet us on some common ground.
You, like us, like Melville, want only bliss
and that's why boys, when they want, should kiss.

In the moment of silence that followed, we kissed, right there, in front of the entire class. A kiss that lasted several moments as Casey geniused a guitar solo. I'd like to think we earned the B+ for that alone.

A Calenture
of the Jungle

AMELIA BELIEVED SHE HAD BEEN BORN without an imagination. She never daydreamed, not even when bored, which she was quite often. While she had loved story time in kindergarten and first grade, she never wanted to read books on her own. Why bother when someone else would do so for you? During school plays, she would sit as close to the stage as possible, but she never even thought of volunteering. Too many lines to remember, too many directions to follow. When she was ten, she discovered she was a glutton for the imagination of others: while watching a DVD at a friend's house, Amelia accidentally sat on the remote control and muted the film; her friend began making voices and dialogue for every character on the television and it was so hilarious. Amelia wanted more.

The day she had her first period and blood stained her underwear, Amelia was given a "talk" by her mother. The "talk" was mind-numbingly boring — Amelia had heard it all before in fifth-grade Human Growth and Change class — until her mom mentioned a scene from some horror novel where a girl was bullied in a locker room shower by her peers who threw tampons at her. *That* should have been a television commercial. *That* was imagination, and every time she inserted that pastel cardboard tube inside her, she thought of that unnamed author of the unread book and hoped she would find someone who would read the story aloud to her.

Dating was neither nightmare nor reverie. She went out with a boys who were either dull, dull, dull or told lies to get at her breasts — small lies for over the shirt, bigger ones for under. Lies should be like a match flame kissing the fuse of dynamite. Boys in high school lived too much in the real world of sweaty locker rooms, fast food, and peeing standing up.

But not the girls. Amelia found that girls, at least, girls interested in other girls, didn't think the same as boys into girls. The girls she made out with still wanted to get their hands under her shirt, but they were honest about it. And so she let them, but even this became boring after a while.

Until she met Stephanie Graveur under the sukkah at a B'nai B'rith Girls Sukkot party.

Her parents were active at synagogue. She went along because there wasn't anything more interesting to do. At least on Saturday mornings she heard parables, which were akin to stories.

Amelia had been at a table handing out flimsy paper cups of bug juice — bright blue and so sweet that yellowjackets committed suicide to get a taste — when Stephanie Graveur stepped ahead of another girl in line and asked for "a dose of poison."

Amelia had heard the word *swoon* before. But never understood it until that moment, when a *swoon* came over her, leaving her flushed and faint, her pulse unsure whether to climb or drop at any moment as she tried to keep the hand holding the plastic ladle steady.

Stephanie's hair was red and she had tucked some bits of palm leaf behind her ear, which should have earned her a lecture from at least someone for being irreverent. A little scar tissue curled the right edge of her mouth. She also kept juggling a couple of lemon-like etrogs.

"You'll spill it. Everywhere," warned some irrelevant adult from nearby.

Stephanie shrugged, tossed one of the fruits high enough it almost broke through the sukkah's flimsy roof, then caught it behind her back. "*She* could hold it for me. Be my right hand gal." A wink at Amelia followed.

Amelia cradled in her hands a very full cup. The liquid inside did look poisonous. Amelia followed Stephanie out into the synagogue's quiet parking lot.

She discovered how hard it is to kiss a juggler intent on not letting anything drop.

After that, Stephanie referred to their meeting as the Cup of Death, as if it was the chapter heading in the story of their first adventure.

Red Caps

AMELIA SUSPECTED STEPHANIE HAD BEEN

born with too much imagination, and whatever nooks and crannies in grey matter held the means for telling stories—and were missing from her own brain—riddled Stephanie's. How else to explain her bedroom? All the walls were decoupaged with four-color comic pages and old movie posters, all the same theme: curvaceous women wearing only animal skins. Some swung on vines, some posed at cave mouths, many held aloft spears or daggers, while defending themselves against wild beasts or savages, as well as hapless white guys in khakis and pith helmets. Jungle girls everywhere.

They were to study Spanish together, but Amelia instead asked Stephanie to read the comics aloud to her. So instead of memorizing *Mas acompañados y pani-aguados debe di tener la locura que la discreción*, Amelia heard *What a lazy day! Go ahead, girls, take a swim. I'll keep an eye open for any danger. You can never tell when it will strike in the jungle!*

One night, after a lively reading which culminated with both girls lying on the carpet, practically under the bed, a bit undressed, a bit out of breath, Stephanie whispered up into Amelia's ear that she wanted to be called Shuka, Guardian of the Jungle.

"And me?" she asked.

"You're Amelia Earhart," Stephanie—no, Shuka—said nuzzling back into Amelia's collarbone. "Your plane crashed in darkest Africa and I found you hanging from your parachute among the trees."

Amelia thought that Earhart had disappeared over the Pacific Ocean, but she remained quiet as Shuka nipped at the sensitive skin of her neck.

"You're an aviatrix." The word sounded exotic. Amelia gasped at where Shuka stroked. "I saved you from danger. Like cannibals and quicksand."

Amelia wanted to nod but, based on how their bodies lay together, she could only press herself tighter against the other girl.

And that was how Amelia Earhart became Shuka's loyal sidekick. And a Game began.

STEPHANIE WOULD HAND A CRYPTIC NOTE

to Amelia in the hall or slip it between the slots of her locker. *The lion sleeps tonight,* read one. *Scoff at the monkeys who live in their dark tents,* another. *Jungle love in the surf in the pouring rain, everything's better when wet* distracted Amelia all day.

When they were alone together, especially outdoors, in the bit of woods left in town, the girls explored the Forbidden City or faced the Phantom Stampede.

Stephanie transformed her emery board and earbuds into a trusty dagger and an ornamental necklace she earned for saving a tribe's sacred white condor from poachers led by an unscrupulous ornithologist. Shuka would stop along the trail to sniff and pronounce, "The smell of gunpowder!" or press an ear to the sidewalk and tell Amelia that "The elephants need help to reach their graveyard."

Amelia did her little part, which was pretty much to stand there, watching a while before asking "How do you know, Shuka?" or "That's amazing."

But the Game had its drawbacks. Last week while showering Amelia had found a relic from their latest romp through the woods: a bloated tick on her upper thigh. Like a wide, black bead piercing her skin. She swallowed a rivulet of coconut-scented shampoo froth at the sight. She scraped it off with a luffa and turned the water to near-scalding as she searched for more, but she still felt ill afterwards. Looking up tick-borne diseases on Wikipedia did not help. Fever? She did feel flushed. Fatigue? She did not want to get out of bed. Depression? She just found a tick inches away from her no-man's land, yes, that was more than depressing!

She texted Stephanie, who came over that night. With a gym bag over her shoulder. "Don't worry. I've seen this before."

Amelia struggled to rise to her elbows in bed, but the many pillows under her head and upper body made it difficult. She wore sweats because they felt comforting. And she was afraid to even glance, even scratch where the tick had been gorging. "You've been bitten?"

Stephanie shook her head. "No. But the Umbati tribe's chief had come down with jungle fever and I helped their witch-doctor acquire all the necessary ingredients for the cure."

Amelia groaned. "I could have...bacteria running rampant inside of me." She covered her face. She must be infected. She was having delusions of her tainted bloodstream, like the educational videos from biology class. Now was not the time for her to develop an imagination.

Stephanie shushed her. And then unzipped the bag and began removing crazy flea-market stuff. A wooden mortar and pestle. A cow horn. A corked bottle. Brittle brown leaves. Little spice jars. She mumbled a wordless chant as she began grinding stuff.

"I should just tell my parents — "

"No!" Shuka slammed the pestle down hard. "The white man's medicine cannot heal you."

"We're both white — " Amelia doubted Stephanie's pale complexion could even sustain a tan.

"Shuka has the soul of darkest Africa."

Amelia groaned.

"This no worse than when Amelia bitten by mamba snake." Shuka poured the dry mix into the wide end of the cow's horn, and then pulled the stopper from the bottle with her teeth.

"That was a scrape on my shoulder after I tripped on a root. And I only went along because you pretended to suck the poison out." Amelia remembered Shuka's warm mouth pressed tight against the sensitive skin just shy of her bra strap.

"Drink."

Amelia clamped her hands over her mouth.

"Is safe." Shuka lifted the horn and took a sip.

Where did the green vapors come from? Amelia's mouth went dry and her temples ached. She must be hallucinating. A disease you could catch from a tick's bite might make you hallucinate. Green vapors do not slip from your girlfriend's mouth like a party trick. Weird green vapors do not rise from a potion in a horn she's forcing you to drink.

"*Drink.*" Shuka knelt on the bed beside Amelia.

The potion smelled like fresh-turned earth, that poignant odor of uncovered mold, of disturbed grubs and worms blended with the sweet scent of torn grass. Amelia accepted the cup, so warm from Shuka's grip that she worried a sip would scald her lips.

She lifted the rim to her own mouth. Shuka watched her with anticipation. Amelia then realized that whatever was inside the horn wasn't medicine – not that she ever believed so – but was a pact. If she wanted to share her life with Stephanie, she would have to prove herself willing to do anything within the Game.

She swallowed and swallowed and refused to dwell on the coarse lumps that threatened to make her gag, that her throat wanted no part of. The taste...her tongue lacked the words, challenged her mind and forced her to imagine the brew was foul, was delicious, tart with loyalty and the aftertaste of devotion.

Shuka kissed away anything that escaped her mouth.

Nighttime, Amelia heard the drums.

Her racing heartbeat, her quickened pulse, she knew, but when she pushed her sweaty head deeper into the pillow, the echo in her ear sounded like drums in the jungle. Her body ached. Her thigh hurt the most, as she had scratched the site of the tick's meal raw again and again, disturbing the scabbing. October

enabled her to hide the bandages she used with leggings, but at school she would slip into the bathroom several times a day, hide in a stall, and scrape her skin.

She dared not tell her parents. They would panic, as they had during the infamous strep-throat outbreak of '11. Her mother would coddle, her father would be stern, and the result of both methodologies would be limiting her time with Stephanie, who had been the one to lure their cherished daughter into the dangerous wilds of suburban New Jersey.

She dared not tell Stephanie. The potion had been bad enough. What would come next?

If only she had a first aid kit. Amelia Earhart must have kept one in the Fokker.

During gym class, she kept to the edges of the field, where the white lines kept the dying grass at bay. Her grip on the hockey stick loose, so much so that it fell from her hand when she spotted in the clear blue sky a vapor trail. Running east, toward Africa, she was sure.

She began hiding the limp that developed a few days later. A bad landing, but one she could walk away from, she told herself. She wasn't feverish but rather inspired. She wanted no distractions from planning for Halloween next week. Not homework, when she needed to be online scouring websites that sold faux-leather aviator caps and goggles. Not school, which she cut one day to get her hair done in the proper bob, then to search thrift stores for a bomber jacket that fit.

Her cell phone became a terrible annoyance with its chirps, toots, whines that weren't even Morse code. It lacked the hiss of static of a radio handset, the cord, and the dials. Months ago she had been thrilled to open the sleek box it came in, marveled at the leather protective sleeve Stephanie had bought her, but now Amelia knew it was worthless in the jungle. She abandoned it when they next played the Game, and grew peeved when Shuka wasted almost two hours searching for it. Amelia pretended to help look, but meanwhile she actually was mapping the terrain in her head. Autumn leaves hid a lot of quicksand in New Jersey.

HER FOREHEAD BURNING, ONE EYE BLIND,
Amelia tried to read the instrument panel but the gauges looked wrong. Fuel, there was fuel, but why was the plane not moving? She undid her harness and opened the cockpit door and collapsed onto asphalt. No, not a runway but a street. She had been at the wheel of her parent's Honda, not her trusty Fokker.

Red Caps

No wonder she had crashed into a sign post. She looked at its warning, *Stop*, and laughed. Nothing stopped Amelia Earhart.

She looked for Shuka. Yelled out her name. Dark shapes began to warily approach from their own stopped cars. Had Shuka been in the passenger seat? Or had the crash happened before Amelia picked her up on the way to Halloween festivities? She remembered they had been talking — arguing — over how little Shuka's leopard-print singlet covered compared to how Amelia was dressed from head to toe. Amelia looked back into the car. Yes, slumped in her seat was her mistress, hair so red, so red, and spilling down over her face. Bejeweled by broken safety glass.

Amelia wiped at her eyes, and her vision returned to the left. Just blood clouding her vision a moment.

The dark shapes around them grew clearer. A gorilla, its head crudely removed and replaced with a television set, antennae extended and awaiting whatever orders its sinister Nazi overlords have planned, shuffled towards her. Not far behind it was some other ghoul.

Smiling, Amelia reached for the pistol inside her bomber jacket. Fresh from the distant Amazon, free two-day delivery, orange like Halloween.

The gorilla stopped in the middle of the street and held up its hands. Good, such a creature still knew fear.

But as she turned around, others were already trying to get to Shuka from her side of the car. Amelia turned the pistol at them, but one had already opened the passenger door.

A spasm of imagination rushed through Amelia; she almost fell from the nausea, the dizziness, its heat. Heroines get captured all the time. She remembered Stephanie reading to her about Princess Pantha being helped by ivory poachers. The sidekick was allowed to rescue the Jungle Girl every few issues. This must be Amelia's story.

She screamed and raised her hand, pulling the trigger. The flare gun coughed and up and up the flare went to explode and turn the night shades of ruby and black. The villains, their pawns, gaped and gasped. While they were distracted, Amelia Earhart ran, into the thick of the jungle. At her back were the cries of predators and cannibals. But she was confident she would return. In the next issue. To save Shuka. She imagined she knew where all the quicksand was.

Three on a Match

A TATTERED BOY NAMED ANTONY SAT ON the unmade dorm room bed rolling a cigarette. His nicotine-stained fingertips maneuvered loose tobacco through the channel made by the curling paper thin as onionskin. The effort left him squinting behind round wire-framed glasses.

The room reeked of tobacco smoke. The ceiling might once have been white, but it and the upper reaches of every wall were tinted an ochery yellow. The naked lamp bulbs accentuated the evidence that a thousand thousand cigarettes had been smoked there.

A wise boy named Ewan leaned against the far wall, close to the door, and watched. His narrow arms were folded, with hands tucked into the warm pockets of his pale blue hoodie. "Anything in that?"

Antony's tongue darted fast to lick the exposed edge of the paper. "Are you worried?"

"I just don't want to be smoking embalming fluid."

"They do that?" Antony finished and then leaned on one elbow while he made the crafted cigarette dance along the tarsals of his hand, like a magician's coin.

"Call 'em 'wets.' Really moronic...and it's all because some idiot confused a nickname for PCP with actual embalming fluid — "

"Where does a guy get his hands on that shit?"

Ewan shrugged. "Formaldehyde's easy to find. Every high school bio lab has jars of the stuff."

"You're really smart, aren't you?" The cigarette stopped moving, pinched tight between Antony's thumb and forefinger.

"Are you flirting?"

"Are you here to get laid?"

"Yes."

Antony's laugh was brief. "Well, that wasn't really flirting. Maybe you're not so smart after all." He reached for the worn leather jacket he had flung onto the bed once they arrived in the bedroom and he retrieved from one pocket a Zippo, its metal skin scratched from many accidents, many falls.

With a practiced ease, Antony flicked the lighter open and thumbed the black wheel. A steady flame grew. "Don't worry. No embalming fluid. No marijuana. Just tobacco supposedly from Turkey, but I suspect really Iowa."

"Didn't think that was a cash crop there." Ewan began to wander the fringes of the dorm room. On top of the dresser he saw ashtrays brimming with the powdered remains. On top of the desk, amid the papers and closed textbooks. Ashes and butts obscured much of Western Civilization.

"Well, that's where the website I bought this stuff is."

"A website isn't anywhere." Ewan lifted one butt, pinched at the end. Let it drop back into the old coffee mug, its home.

"Sure it is."

"No, it doesn't take up physical space. It's in the..." Ewan gestured. His fingernails were scored, bitten down to the quick, stained brown from dried blood, not yellow like the other boy's.

"Æther?"

"Yeah, guess you could call it that. What you mean is the company is based in Iowa. Or maybe the servers."

Antony lit one end of the cigarette, and then motioned with that hand. "Come here."

"My breath probably smells like beer." Ewan covered his mouth with his fingertips a moment. Ran his tongue along his front teeth.

"This will cure that."

Ewan walked across the room, avoiding the piles of discarded clothes and crumb-covered plates. He sat down at the foot of the bed. He curled an arm around the nearest of the wooden knobs of the footboard.

Red Caps

Antony put the cigarette to his mouth and inhaled. The lit end blossomed in oranges dying to black and gray that fell like snow onto his worn Red Caps concert T-shirt. The ash drifted across the faded lettering.

"I know a trick," Antony whispered.

Ewan leaned in closer. "A magic trick?"

"There's no other worth knowing." He handed the cigarette over. "Do you want to see it?"

"I thought we were going to..."

"Fuck?"

Ewan winced at the word but nodded. He inhaled deeply the smoke a moment, then let it stream through his nostrils as if he were an irate cartoon bull. Or some ancient idol found in a fiery cave.

"If that word scares you...this trick would make you lose your shit. Maybe you should run back to high school."

Ewan dropped his cigarette. Both boys scrambled through the loose and dirty sheets to retrieve it before it scorched the bedding. Their hands mingled and slapped and stroked one another in the process.

Antony recovered the cigarette and handed it back. "Newb."

He started rolling another cigarette. "The more smoke, the better my trick. Sometimes I just buy packs 'cause it's easier, faster. Has to be Lucky Strikes though. No other brand works. But I can leave them burning in an ashtray and... well, you'll see."

Ewan adjusted the front of his jeans as he watched the other boy.

Once their mouths were occupied by purported Turkish tobacco and releasing streams of blue-gray vapor, Antony began rubbing Ewan's knee through the faded denim.

"I'm addicted."

"To these?"

Antony shook his head. "No, to a ghost. Or maybe he's made of æther. You'll see." He let his hands roam higher until they slid across the soft material of the hoodie, and then he began pushing against the other boy's chest. Gently to start, then more firmly.

Ewan slid back but Antony kept forcing him further until he had met the edge of the bed.

"The floor?"

"Trust me." Antony smirked. "Isn't it so late that you're too tired to do anything else but trust me?"

Arms lifted like ballet dancers to keep their smokes safe, they tumbled to the cheap, industrial carpet. A glimpse under the bed revealed even more full ashtrays, the discarded cellophane from countless Lucky Strikes packs. Dead matches, resembling the burnt limbs of spiders.

"Ever been in love?" Antony asked.

"Once. Or I thought I was."

Antony blew a series of smoke rings that mimicked his rounded lips. But the rings soon bloated and warped as if under a breeze that stole its way into the college dorm room, stole its way without ever being felt. They drifted one after another to the air above the bed. Ewan moved, leaning up on his elbows, to watch his own tobacco breath stream after the misshapen rings, even when he tried to blow smoke off to his left, to his right, down into his palm.

"Me too." Antony frowned. "Even if I'm with other boys, I need *him* to be there. I don't hook up unless I bring them back here." He gestured at the cloud of smoke somewhat visible from where both boys lay. Floating inches above the mattress an unfashioned figure was being born.

"I've wondered if maybe he's a boy who once went to school here. Not like I'm a detective, not like there's anyone to ask. And I'm not even sure I really want to know who he was. That would destroy the mystery. You need mystery to make a magic trick work."

Ewan almost stumbled as he stood. "Have you named him?" Another deep inhalation, release, and he watched as the smoke drifted down, layering onto the floating mass. Features developed but the whole remained a crude sculpture of redolent fumes with a suggestion of youth despite the square jaw. No fingers, no lines of clothing, no shoes or toes.

Antony stood beside Ewan. Rubbed his back, let his hand slide down and grabbed hold of his ass. "I call him Beauty." His voice sounded raspy, as if those thousand thousand cigarettes had, at last, eaten away the soft, warm lining of the boy's throat. "I never want to leave him."

"Has he ever spoken?"

"No."

"Woken?"

Antony sighed. "Maybe he isn't sleeping."

Ewan walked to and fro beside the bed. Like a skeptical member of a magician's audience he passed first a hand and then a pillow between the sleeping beauty and the mattress.

"We should smoke more. I want to see him whole," he said.

Antony went for the Lucky Strikes, though their odor was comparable to coffee left on the burner rather than the scent conjured by the loose tobacco.

"When you bring back boys, do you make them kiss him too?"

Antony hesitated as he lit the first three cigarettes on the same flame. "Bad luck three on a match I heard, but don't know why. But yeah..."

"Why? And how many are cool with that?"

"I thought maybe he'd wake up. I've given up my lungs to make him appear. What more can I do? Maybe I'm not a Prince, not Charming enough. Or whatever works with magic these days. Probably needs someone pure or sweet."

"And I seem like either?" Ewan offered a slight smile but stepped close to accept a Lucky Strike.

"Most guys balk at even the talk of magic tricks. They think it's slang for meth bumps up the ass or something."

Ewan looked back at floating Beauty. Wavy locks of hair had developed. A slender nose. Closed eyelids. Ewan leaned in close and exhaled over where the mouth should be and waited as thin lips, parted ever so slightly, coalesced.

"Any guy stay?"

"Once. I think he was on E. His teeth chattered as we messed around and I found him in the morning down the hall in the bathroom drinking out of the sink like a weird pet."

"So not the sort of ménage à trois you wanted."

"No. Beauty didn't stir." Antony stepped behind Ewan, their torsos touching, older boy's chin resting on the younger's shoulder. He slid a hand down the front of Ewan's jeans, between denim and cotton underwear. Fingers curled.

A hitch in Ewan's breathing. "There's another boy at school that everyone knows is gay. My dad's a teacher, so they leave *me* alone, but this boy...they pounce on his every move. He can't go anywhere without hearing the word 'Faggot.' If he fights back, he earns a black eye. Or a suspension.

"One day he texts me — took me a while to figure out it was him, as I didn't have his number on my phone, that shows you how close we were — and tells me he's going to kill himself."

Antony's hand stopped moving. He whispered in Ewan's ear, "Damn."

"Yeah. I didn't know what to do. Do I call nine-one-one? I didn't even know where he lived. I try to talk him out of it, then go through the loops — friends of friends of friends, which takes forever, to find his address. The way only seventeen minutes can feel like forever.

"I drive there. The house is dark. No car in the driveway, but I can hear the engine's heartbeat behind the garage door. He left the front door open. He wanted to be found."

"What did you do?"

"I went inside. Found the door to the garage. I know you can't smell carbon monoxide. Can't see it, yet I was disappointed as I opened that door. I expected to see..." Ewan gestured around himself with his hands, one trailing a stream of smoke from cigarette to Beauty, like an umbilical cord.

"And?" Antony squeezed the hardness beneath his hand. Ewan gasped.

"And the boy who planned to die is lying on the hood of his beat-up car. As if he were out in the woods and stargazing. He turned to me and nodded as if I weren't interrupting anything special.

"Which is why...which is why I didn't even cough — there was as much carbon monoxide in the garage as there is here, from our cigs — and I scooched over onto the hood beside him.

"When I turn to talk to him, he brings a hand over my mouth — "

"Like this?" Antony brought up his other hand, the one with a lit cigarette, and held it close to Ewan's lips. As Ewan inhaled from the older boy's cigarette, he thrust an eager crotch against a wanting hand.

"And...and...then he leans over and kisses me. First time I ever kissed a boy."

"And neither of you died?" asked Antony, who continued stroking.

"No, my kiss was magic...the magic trick. We both lived. Lived to see the paramedics arrive."

Warmth spilled over Antony's fingers and soaked the cotton. Ewan stumbled forward.

Antony maintained his hold for a bit longer, then slid his hand from the younger boy's pants. He dropped his lit cigarette into the nearest ashtray and wiped his hand dry on his shirt.

"Will you kiss him? Kiss Beauty? Maybe you can bring him back — "

Ewan curled his lips. "You haven't even kissed me yet."

"Not yet." Antony took the inches of cigarette from him and pressed chapped lips against chapped lips. Teeth tapped and sour tongues explored.

Arms lifted, hands tugged at clothes. Shirts lifted, layers peeled away, denim dragged down and off stick legs.

The carpet chafed exposed skin.

Antony cried out, "Please."

Ewan did not release his hold until the other boy pleaded, ordered, begged. Stroking became fumbling as they stripped each other bare of the many layers of clothing. Faces roamed over bodies. Saliva and sweat mixed and the taste in both their mouths was flavored by old spilled ashes.

When naked Antony rolled off bared Ewan, the latter said, "He's gone," and pointed one scrawny arm towards the mattress. With its mess of stained sheets, it looked like so many other boys' beds.

"He was never here. Remember? A trick. To get laid. Smoke and mirrors."

"I think you're lying."

Antony shrugged.

"No Beauty?"

Antony stared at Ewan. "Maybe some." He stroked a cheek, ran his fingers down the curve of neck.

Ewan closed his eyes. "My trick's no better than yours. Actually mine is far, far worse."

Antony pressed a thumb against the corner of Ewan's mouth and made the lips pout.

"When I opened the door to the garage, I choked on the fumes. Had to turn my head. I was only smart enough to flick every switch, so the garage door went up but the lights came on and I saw him there, saw him lying on the roof of his car but his eyes stared up at nothing.

"I tried to wake him. Slapped his face. Even kissed him like they do in movies and television, but nothing happened. He didn't wake."

Antony edged closer so there was no distance between their limbs, their feverish skin. "So we're both liars."

"Smoke and mirrors." Ewan ran a hand through Antony's hair. "At least tell me your name."

FOR ALEX

Steeped in Debt to the Chimney-pots

"A friendly sprite whispered in his ear, and saved him from too utter folly.
The sprite had not yet forsaken him; woe to him if ever it should!"
— George Gissing, *Thyrza*

Winter, 1884

ATOP THE COLD, BRONZE SHOULDER OF
his favorite statue in Hyde Park, a sprite watched the sun die across the sky. He
had spent the day tallying the debts still owed on twelve fingers and toes and
the result saddened him. Freedom was an illusion — what he owed to the other
Folk who were insane enough to make sick London their home would keep him
bound to the city for years. The Folk had a code: nothing could be freely given
or expected and words had to be measured, worried over. Tupp Smatterpit envied humans and had grown fond of mortal pubs where he saw drinks bought
because one man's fortune inclined him to generosity, a word the Folk had forgotten. Or maybe his kith were unable to share true good will and affection.

Thoughts of debts and affections made him envision Lind. Tupp wondered
why he found the human lad's foolhardiness so appealing.

Tupp tossed his hat, aiming for the bronze sword. It landed at the base of the statue's stone pedestal. He held his breath, expecting a late carriage to come along and trample the hat beneath iron-shod hooves.

Addressing the statue, "What binds you, friend? Poured and cast aside...where's my luck, why only this folly?" Tupp stroked the handsome metal face. He had come to admire a few manmade works about London, especially this statue in the park, an ancient warrior, bared muscular arms and torso that required the severity and strength of metal as their form. Perhaps this was modeled after another creature of legend; Tupp often daydreamed atop the statue that such men still walked secret lands.

But now his fancy was confined to his partner in crime. Tupp closed his eyes and envisioned Lind's features cast in bronze: that sharp nose and those small eyes so quick to hide beneath greasy locks. A bit of hair on his chin. No sculptor ever let a masterpiece wear such a wide grin. No, statues are solemn, a word that Tupp doubted Lind even knew.

And how would Lind react if he ever discovered Tupp's idle longing? If only affection could be freely given, freely returned between Folk and man.

Tupp's ears picked up the sound of footfalls on the icy grass. He looked down to see a small figure wearing so long a scarred leather vest that it threatened to trip him. A cobbler to the Folk. A leprechaun with tufts of white hair growing long from his ears.

"You're the one they says is payin' for that rapparee's deeds."

Tupp sighed and nodded. Just how many of the Folk had Lind robbed? Tupp leapt down from the statue and picked up his hat.

"Then you're a gowl to be handin' out glamour to save a human's hide."

Tupp reached into his waistcoat pocket and removed a snuffbox. Once it had been full of glittering, golden powder — glamour, what kept Iron Sickness at bay and allowed the Folk to disguise themselves. He opened the lid. Barely more than two pinches remained. He offered one to the leprechaun.

He harrumphed as he took his due. "In my day, any mortal so bold as to steal from our kind, we'd make him dance still his soles bled. I could make him a pair of brogues that would clench his feet like a dog's jaw."

"No," Tupp said. "He's mine. So his debts are mine to pay."

THOUGH HE HAD NO WATCH, LIND KNEW HE was late in meeting his partner in crime, Tupp. As he lost his last farthing the bell of some nearby church had tolled five o'clock. The winter sun set and Lind stood among grimy boys — costers and shoeblacks, broomers and runners, poor streetlarks all — huddled beside an old coal barge. Though stuck fast for years in the Thames mud, the barge offered protection from both the brutal wind and the wandering eyes of any constable.

Lind shuddered beneath his greatcoat. He should never have spent the day gambling. First the worst of luck at cards, then wagering over how many chops a man could eat, then this, the lowest, emptying his pockets at three-up — a child's game, tossing pennies high and wagering on whether they came down heads or tails.

Thirteen shillings gone. Thirteen shillings, yesterday's take from selling a hob's loot to Kapel. Lind could suffer the pain of losing his own coin — it happened often enough — but to gamble away Tupp's share? He worried how the sprite would react. Would his customary cheer falter? Would he curse Lind?

A sliver of a boy dashed from the direction of the docks and yelled out, "Traps comin'!" the crowd scattered fast. Lind climbed the derelict barge. Coal dust from the old wood rubbed off on his palms, reminding him of a childhood spent with soot covering every inch of him. He should be running off, but he dawdled, wondering if time spent in prison would be a safer life. The Folk hated iron. Bars might keep them away.

But no constable came. Lind realized that it had all been a cheat, that one or more of the streetlarks must have pocketed the brass and run while the others fled. He looked out at the shoreline, lit by fading sunlight, and spotted three figures running together. One carried a broom: the sweep who'd collected the wagers.

He could follow them. Demand a share of the take. He jumped down onto the shore. The river's muck tried to steal his shoes. He felt the chill reach his stockings as he pried his feet lose and ran after them. Pale faces turned back. With a cry, the three splintered. Lind followed the one with the broom.

The boy headed for a dark blotch in the distance, one that grew distinctive as Lind ran. Another dock, one so dilapidated, like a carcass picked clean at the dinner table, the askew pilings might have been rib bones of some great beast.

Cold air was quick to constrict Lind's lungs, and he had to catch his breath at the first piling. The sun had set, leaving little light to see by. So he blinked in disbelief when a weak flame answered his need. Where the black water lapped the shore, a bedraggled figure held aloft a candle lantern. A mudlark? They searched the Thames muck for rubbish that washed ashore. But where was her hamper? And why would she be out so late?

"Lost boy." The mudlark spoke with a country accent, of lush green grass that bent beside the river. The image of gentle ripples on the water filled his head, and, despite the cold, he began to relax against the piling. "Come, let me take you home," she said.

The harsh wind brought to Lind the smell of something dredged from the dark bottom of the filthy Thames, and he fought the urge to retch. Then he glimpsed the mudlark's face: wet hair clung to gaunt features and empty eye sockets; the squat green teeth within her long jaws belonged to a drowned mule, not any woman. Fear surpassed the bile in his throat. It seeped out through the pores of his skin on rivulets of sweat. He *knew* her. He shivered and slipped around the piling so she could not see him. "Jenny," he whispered.

Months ago, after some mishaps that nearly ended with him being caught, Lind had stopped robbing houses. Why risk the noose? That was when he started stealing from the Folk. The small ones. Goblins mostly. A cobbler with odd ears. What harm could they do to him? And they would never talk to a human magistrate and risk revealing their presence in the city. It was all so easy.

Until he made a terrible mistake. From the safety of a rooftop, Lind had watched one of the Folk sink a net fashioned from rags down an old well. While she looked hideous, he never thought her truly dangerous. So after she'd left, he climbed down the slimy walls and recovered a silver hand mirror and matching hairbrush. The find made him laugh — why would something so ugly keep mementoes belonging to a lady, not a frow? Even dry, the handles kept her stink, so Kapel, his favorite fence, had refused to offer a fair price for either.

But when he started working with the sprite Tupp, selling recovered glamour to the Folk so they could survive the pains that living in London brought — all that smoke, all that worked iron — Lind discovered that goblins talked, that word had spread of a brazen human stealing from them. And that Green Jenny liked to drown her victims. Before she ate them.

Lind glanced around the rotting wooden piling. He saw the sweep stepping out from under the dock toward her. The boy wore a smile, which chilled Lind worse than Jenny's terrible face. Glamour hid her true visage from the boy. Lind could not see the lacquer, whatever beauty and cheer she masked herself with. He'd been a child when soot dislodged by a brownie had fallen into his eyes and cursed him with the Sight.

No one deserved Jenny's fatal embrace, but Lind didn't dare risk his own life to save the poor bloke. He imagined her sharp fingers clutching at his coat's sleeve as they dragged him towards the water. The Thames would be so icy and dark, blinding him to everything but her face as he choked on the river water.

No, not even the promise of a hundred shillings in the sweep's pockets could move Lind. He pressed his back to the pylon and told himself that cowards live longer than heroes. In his head, Lind said the only prayer he knew, a Hebrew one for blessing wine that Kapel had taught him.

Perhaps the Thames was so cold that it would stop the boy's heart before Jenny began stroking his hair. Lind caught a weak voice calling out, "Mum?" He hoped he misheard and the sound was just the wind.

FEW TAPMEN IN LONDON POUR A CHARITY

mug for a stranger, so Lind, desperate to get good and drunk, had to be watchful at Boniface's tavern, where he always met Tupp. When he saw an old man slouch beside his drink, he came close. There was more than enough gin left in the cup to swallow, and it was the proper duty of every Englishman to see that nothing went to waste in the Empire. When the bloke's trembling eyelids shut, Lind lifted the tin cup from the scarred table.

Lind scraped the mud from his shoes on the bulldog-shaped andirons set in the fireplace. A fire had consumed much of the log. He couldn't rid his soul of the cold left from seeing Jenny. Before he could finish off that sip of gin, a pearl-gray top hat, a bit battered, landed over the cup's mouth.

"There's no more welcome sign of winter than a trio of hags roastin' chestnuts." With a grin tight between ruddy and round cheeks, Tupp scampered up and onto the mantelpiece.

The handsome sprite wore a fustian coat the shade of caked mustard and a loose blue cravat that drooped around his neck. A child clown would envy those clothes, but no one in Boniface's laughed at Tupp. Grains of glamour kept the crowd from noticing the odd outfit, not to mention Tupp's crescent-shaped ears and the six slender fingers on both hands. "Mind you, only buy them from the youngest, the maiden, as the meat's the sweeter." Tupp reached over and lifted his hat up. Somehow, in doing so, he stole the tin cup from Lind's hand. He drained its contents quick, then tossed it into the fireplace where it made embers rise and dance a while.

"If you're so happy for winter, let's toast to it. Buy us a drink." Lind wished he could laugh then and there at Tupp, who often acted mad as a spoon. A cherished, heirloom spoon.

"And the nuts in the crone's pan might be a touch...morbose." Tupp started pressing out the many dents in the brim of his hat.

Lind rubbed at his throat and coughed. "Some drink to fend off the ague I feel risin' — "

Tupp bit down on the brim a moment, then seemed satisfied. To Lind, the hat still looked to be the same sorry shape. Tup placed it atop his auburn curls with a rakish slant. "Why are your pockets are empty? Didn't you see your Hebrew?"

"I-I.... No. I'll go tomorrow."

"Just as well. We will have something else for him. Tonight."

Lind wanted to stay with the drunks — the elbow-crookers, he liked to call them — at Boniface's until he was thoroughly pissed. He did not want another glimpse through the strange keyhole of weird. "Could we not stay here? Or, fine, somewhere else. Just the two of us." He put a hand over Tupp's. "There's mischief we can share rather than work another night." But Lind could not bring himself to ask Tupp to indulge in the real mischief he truly wanted to share with the sprite.

He hoped that Tupp would see in his eyes that Lind wanted no more selling powdered glamour to the scrambling child with sharp claws that clung beneath the eaves of St. Giles' Ragged School. No more silent women laundering mounds of bloody clothes in the dark at the Poplar Hospital for Accidents. Once it had been exciting, as if he had learned the greatest cheat in all the world, but now the wonder turned to horror.

Tupp frowned. "If only we could. But I have debts to pay."

"One night? They won't forgive one night?"

Tupp dropped to his feet. "A brisk walk will do us well."

Lind rubbed the disappointment from his face. He understood how avoiding debts only brought misery...that, and he did not trust most of the Folk Tupp dealt with — on his own, they would cheat the sprite out of glamour without a second thought.

No matter how fresh the snow, the cobblestones of London turned it filthy. Nimble Tupp walked atop the ashen broth. Lind never saw him slip and envied the sprite's dry feet. By the time they had walked several blocks, Lind was shivering, his feet soaked. He asked Tupp if they could hire a cab.

But Tupp refused to spare even a farthing. "Nonsense demands."

Lind groaned. Why did only mortals suffer from nonsense?

They came to a corner with a coffee-stall flickering light and warmth from its lit fire-pan. The smell rising from the pot tugged at Lind's empty stomach. "A mug would warm the insides," he said. "Please, Tupp."

"That it would," said the stall-keeper. "Best thing for you now."

Then Lind spied a set of scrawny limbs covered in ragged clothing move in the shadows of the doorway just behind the stall. He felt the flush of panic seize him. Had Jenny ventured out of the frigid Thames for him? But then he saw the faces of the women who stepped into the fire-pan's glow. Weak-eyed and wan but decidedly human.

"Lind, we don't want to keep this one waiting long," Tupp said. "He's a most sallow fellow."

Lind thought all of the Folk were sallow. 'Cept Tupp, who possessed a grin and a wink.

The taller of the women moved next to Lind. Her sunken cheeks told of too many hungry nights. "Spare a penny for me and my sister to warm ourselves? Terrible cold out."

A soft chime sounded from Tupp's waistcoat. Tupp muttered as he consulted one of his many pocket watches.

Lind didn't put much weight on education; how'd reading ever save a man's life? But he knew that the queer markings on the watch's face didn't match any English numbers or letters. Didn't look Hebrew either.

"A pretty," said the second woman, who leaned down to dislodge Tupp's hat and finger his copper curls. "'Ave time for me, 'an'som?"

Lind wondered how she noticed Tupp; he should have been dusted with glamour and hidden from sight, as he had been at the pub. Had the sprite become careless? Had the pinch worn off?

Tupp ignored the woman. "I smell currant cake." He slipped the watch back into a pocket and retrieved his hat from the ground.

Lind saw the greed in the woman's eyes. He understood the promise of gold, the promise of trouble. But it would not end well for the women. Tupp might curse them to wander all night long till they dropped from the cold. Not that Lind had ever seen the sprite do so, but he had overheard Tupp threaten others he *could*.

"Let's be going," Lind said.

"A bit o' that cake would be nice."

"Like sweets?" The one woman stopped down to rub at Tupp's belly. She whispered in his ear while her fingers slipped towards the waistcoat pocket with the watch.

"I prefer cakes to tarts." Tupp's elbow struck her in the chest. She shrieked and fell into the snowbroth.

"'Ere now," called out the stall keeper. First his pockmarked cheeks and then his chest puffed in readiness, like rising hackles on an angry mutt.

"No," Lind shouted and reached for the fire-pan's handle. Pulled loose of the stall, it fell to the wet cobblestones and rolled, spilling hot coals that steamed and hissed as they died.

Red Caps

The women screamed, the stall keeper cursed, but Lind grabbed Tupp by his collar and pulled him down the street at a run. When the cold air burned inside Lind's chest, they took refuge in an alley. Lind gasped for breath. "No more," he panted to Tupp, who leaned against the opposite brick wall and regarded him with curiosity.

"But you haven't had a taste yet." Tupp held up a stolen currant cake.

"What next?"

"Hmmm?"

Lind rubbed both palms against his watery eyes, wishing he could wipe away the Sight. He wanted nothing more to do with the Folk. Even Tupp was too dangerous to associate with...and yet he did not want to abandon the sprite.

When he looked up, he saw Tupp had grown a foot taller and stood beside him. Tupp blew hard over the cake before breaking it in half. "You asked me to be partners. Now you have regrets?"

"Every day, every hour, I feel as if I'm risking everything, but I have nothing to show for it."

"Nothing? You're with me," Tupp said.

"And you're the only thing keeping me from going mad."

"Shhhh," Tupp whispered. "I'd not say that. The Folk like their mortals mad."

The cake smelled like spring, like how gold should smell. Spit filled Lind's mouth. He took the offered half, noted how it was warm to the touch as if baked within the half hour. Grit met his teeth at the first bite, and then such sweetness overcame his tongue. Lighter than treacle. Lighter than honey. He couldn't bring himself to chew fast enough so he swallowed fast, as fever spread through him. He felt a bead of sweat start at his temple — or perhaps it was a tear traveling down his cheek — drifting down, along the path to the scar at his chin, where it was damned to freeze. He didn't know why he'd be crying. He didn't have a worry to his name.

The currants cradled in his five fingers went from wine-red to glittering amber. No, gold, like Tupp's watches. Lind started chuckling like some fresh-faced sot. Treasure had been within those women's reach all the time; all they needed to do was pull apart the cake.

"Laughter's better than melancholy," offered Tupp, staring at him while nibbling his share.

Lind nodded, though he didn't understand what Tupp meant. He stuffed the rest of the cake into his mouth, and then wiped the greases from his fingers onto his coat. Reckless thoughts murmured in the corners of his head. Break into some fancy's tall house and steal a billiards table. Or climb a gaslight pole and wait for the first carriage to pass beneath and jump down into the coachman's bench. Or remain in the alley and brush the crumbs from Tupp's lips.

He took a step closer to the sprite. Kissing one of the Folk would be the most enchanting thing. And so he did. Press his lips against Tupp's. He curled his fingers around Tupp's lapels, opened his mouth to compare the sweetness of cake to that of sprite.

Then sudden pain ripped at his guts. Lind bent over, clutching at his stomach. The kiss forgotten. He was so empty, so hollow, as if he'd never swallowed a morsel of food in his life. When had he last eaten? Days? No, it felt more like weeks ago. Starving, he scraped at the cobblestones for whatever grime he could lift on his finger.

TUPP REGRETTED CHARMING LIND. HE

only wanted to see him smile and laugh. Then the kiss...how long ago had been the last time he kissed another? If he could not remember, then too long. But was the kiss freely given? Was a kiss bought by too much ale the same as one given by magic?

Tupp had not anticipated how fragile Lind had become. He had to forcibly lift the lad up from the ground, restrain him from filling his mouth with dirt and frozen water. Lind's sense of daring had cracked like old lacquer. Might there be anything left even if Tupp did manage to satisfy all the Folk the lad had wronged?

When they reached Gilspir Street, the famine in Lind's gullet had faded to a distant echo. Tupp doffed his hat at the gilded cherub roosting above on the Fortune of War's outer wall. Inside, the taproom reeked of harsh tobacco, burnt grease, and stale, spilt beer. Tupp led the way through the crowd towards a bench set against the far wall, where a bony fellow, face hidden under his wide-brimmed black hat, sat hunched in whispers to a swarthy bloke with greasy hair falling into his eyes.

"Eur Du's an ankou, a gloomy lot," Tupp whispered to Lind. "When the sun's up, he works as a mute at funerals, walking in the train, dressed all in black. But moonlight brings out his true nature. Before the earth settles on a grave, he's digging it back open. None sacks a corpse faster than Eur Du."

THE BONY MAN LIFTED A HAND TO BECKON

them closer. The unkempt bloke snatched a sack from the floorboards, glared at Lind, and then left. Tupp sat down in his place.

"So the sprite brought his foundlin'." Air whistled past the remains of Eur Du's nose and made his thick accent all the harder to understand.

"We're partners." Lind forced himself to meet the ankou's gaze. Eur Du sounded French and looked pox-riddled as well. Perhaps the Continent was also infested with goblins.

"Of course." A hand scratched the ragged hole below his narrowed dark eyes. "Manee interestin' dealin's happen here. Do you know this place's historee?"

Lind sighed. Why did all the Folk waste so much time dwelling on the past? Yesterday belonged to bad dreams. Greed demanded the mind stay sharp and consider tomorrow's worth.

"No? Bodee snatchers favored this house. Resurrectionists. They'd prop all the bodees on these benches 'round the walls. Had the owner's name underneeth. Wouldn't bee the leest surprise if right under your ass there might been a corpse."

Something grabbed hold of Lind's ankle, freezing skin and bone. He cried out and the patrons of the Fortune of War looked up from their mugs to mutter and stare.

Eur Du's and Tupp's laughter made his face flush. Pranks annoyed Lind unless they were meant as a distraction before a theft. Tupp's amusement felt like a stab in Lind's back.

"So you have...?" Eur Du asked.

Tupp grinned and took from his waistcoat pocket a scrap of newspaper. His nimble fingers unfolded an advertisement for replacement teeth that held a pinch of golden powder settling into the creases. Glamour. The dust every Folk in London needed. Not only to disguise their presence but to fend off iron-sickness as well.

The ankou leaned forward. His breath stank like spoiled meat, and Lind wondered how much of the tavern's stench began with Eur Du. "Is *mad*, is good."

Lind slid the paper way from Eur Du. "Now, your offer?"

The ankou lifted his hat. Fine white hairs, perhaps cobwebs, covered his speckled pate where he kept safe a jeweled ring, which he lifted loose and set on Tupp's open palm.

"As you say, is good." Tupp turned the ring so the smaller red stones sparkled around their older brother. Then he passed it on to Lind. The silver band was cold to his fingers, as if freshly dug from the mounds of snow outside. Or the hard, frozen earth. He imagined Eur Du at work with his shovel, prying at a coffin much as a hungry man would take a knife to a closed oyster.

"Get us drinks, sprite."

Tupp hesitated a moment, then headed for the taps.

Eur Du scraped free a flake of skin hanging from his cheek with one cracked nail. "Eur Du can smell death as perfume. You wear it. Old. Your mother, yes? Bringin' you into the world took her out, yes? That makes you start life a murderer. Eur Du respect that."

Lind slid a hand into his coat and gripped the handle of his knife. Now he hated this one. Perhaps all the Folk. He imagined plunging the iron blade once, twice, into Eur Du's chest.

"But then," the ankou muttered as a black ribbon around his hat rose like a threatened serpent, "all your kind die so easilee, so fast. If I do not see you tomorrow, I assume you dead."

Lind reached for the glamour, folding the edges of the newspaper shut. "Best enjoy this. You'll not see another pinch more from us."

A chuckle wheezed through Eur Du's tiny, sharp teeth. "Do you reelee think he will keep you well, brammig? We may not be able to utter untruths but know that we can never be trusted. When you no longer amuse the sprite, he will forsake you." The ankou's arm shot forth and covered Lind's hand with its own, a leathery touch that masked an iron grip. "An' then, we'll be waitin'."

Lind managed to slip his hand free. Small grains of earth clung to the lines of his knuckles. Grave mold, he was sure. "You think I trust Tupp? You're wrong, bogey. I know he'll soon be bored of me." He made a show of turning away from the ankou to hide his lie. He watched Tupp carry mugs in each hand. Tupp wore his usual grin, which, for a moment, softened the growing hardness in Lind's chest. For a moment. Then Lind slid the knife out of his pocket and opened the blade. "I'm expecting your lot as well." He hoped his hand did not shake as he stabbed the blade down hard in the wood, a splinter's length away from Eur Du's fingers.

Before Tupp set the mugs on to the

table, he waited for Lind to pry loose the knife and return it to his coat. He smirked. So not all Lind's bluster was gone. Tupp lifted up his hat to reveal a third mug, which he set in front of Lind.

"So we have a deal, Eur Du?" he asked.

The ankou nodded as he slid the glamour close.

The watered beer tasted sour, as if the stink in the ankou's hair had settled on the drink's surface. Tupp started pouring out his mug on to the floorboards and Lind was swift to catch as much of the stream in his own emptied mug. "Why waste beer on haunts?" Lind said while staring at Eur Du.

Red Caps

Out on the street, Tupp turned to Lind. "I've some errands. We'll divide the take tomorrow night. At the Bridge of Sighs." He took a few steps, remembered that he had traded away his last pinch of glamour, and then turned back. "And bring the rest of the glamour."

"What? Why?"

The Folk cannot lie. The words cannot leave their mouth. They remain trapped in the imagination. And so he could only say, "Because I have no more of my own."

"But you kept more than me."

"Would you have all of London see me?" Tupp asked.

"How do I know who might see you when I have no idea where you go? Errands. Always errands. I want one night to spend together, but you always run from me."

"I'm not sure you know what you want of me."

Lind opened his mouth, then covered it with one palm, as if stifling his words. Perhaps, Tupp wondered, mortals could not tell the truth. "Nothing. Go. Tomorrow at the bridge."

Not every one of the Folk inside London despised or preyed mortals. One spent most of his time beneath the ground, within the environs of the massive tunnel running underneath the Thames.

It took Tupp a while to find the bluecap tapping at the walls. His calling out "Firma" startled the fairy. Firma blinked its enormous lantern-like eyes. It dropped a small pick and clutched the soiled cap from its head, revealing a corona of pale blue flames rather than hair.

"Few sprites venture down here, Smatterpit."

"Yes." He had never sold glamour to Firma. Bluecaps rarely were seen by miners or diggers. And if they were, it was welcome because they were seen as warning mortals of unsafe conditions. But they had crossed paths before, years ago, and Tupp knew that Firma was one of the very few Folk in London to have kept a mortal lover for decades.

"I need a favor."

The bluecap coughed. Or maybe giggled. "None of the Folk come to me for... for anything."

"I cannot offer much — "

"What favor?"

"Tell me how you have kept your mortal happy for so long."

"Bessie." Firma smiled. "She has burrowed into my heart. I'd not have it any other way."

"But she will die. You will go, but she will die. How can it be more than just some grand banquet, enjoyed for a brief time, but then — "

"But you always remember the banquet. Each course remains with you no matter how you pick away at the plate. I'd not want to miss the meal for fear of the bill." Firma patted Tupp on the shoulder. "Loving anything is not about possessing it. See," he said and reached down for a clod of earth. "I love this dirt, this earth, this England. But do I own it? No. I am merely passing my way through it, and it meets my touch and sight and smell — " Firma breathed in the dirt " — for a moment. A moment I can cherish or not, but why not cherish then?"

Tupp nodded and this new-found wisdom. "My debt — "

"You owe me nothing."

"But...but...that is not how we do things." He did not know how to react to generosity.

"You asked me how I have kept my Bessie happy, it is also because I give freely."

"Then I should do the same," Tupp said and realized there was another of the Folk he had to see, to talk to, that night.

Hot brickwork burned Lind's palms

and knees. Weak light, distant above, teased his eyes. The air tasted heavy with ash, cousin to the soot that blackened every inch of stone and skin and forced him to breath through his nose or gag and choke. He inched upwards along the tight throat of the chimney, then stopped. As a gangly ten year old, Lind had easily scurried up tight passages, but it had been six years since last he swept, and a diet of stout and meat had filled out his frame. He found himself wedged tight.

Angry whispers began where he should be alone. Clearing soot was silent, awful work. After the first bitter mouthful, climbing boys kept lips pressed tight unless they dared to call for help. He clawed at the rough edges to push himself towards the roof.

A rough voice from the drawing room below echoed in the chimney like a dog's barking. Mr Barling demanding Lind climb higher. The whispers became titters. Something sharp bit at the soles of his bare feet. Mr Barling must have borrowed a hatpin from the missus, perhaps the one with a gaudy faux pearl at the end. A lit match would be next.

Lind struggled but could not inch higher. His lungs ached for a good breath. He knew that if he started to panic, the walls of the chimney would seem to draw closer. Beneath him, the stream of curses came faster and higher-pitched, as if the other sweeps giggled at the fireplace's mouth.

Fresh pain along his shins stirred Lind. He blinked at the sunlight that slipped through drapes encrusted with dust and grime. Morning in the room he rented at the end of New Lent Road. He dreamt too often of the past, as if his sleeping thoughts regretted ever running away from Barling's basement.

He tried to wipe the nightmare from his face but found he could not raise a hand. Another binding pulled taut around his neck.

First he cursed, then he struggled more.

The same titters from his dream sounded around the room. Soft as a whisper till they deepened to a final gurgle, the laugh of infants. His vision restrained, Lind glimpsed several small shapes scurrying by the cracked plaster walls, around the ends of the drapes, near the mattress. Rats didn't move on two legs. Rats didn't stink like a heap of soft apples.

"Out! Out," Lind screamed and heaved hard against whatever strings or cords tied him down.

Something landed on his stomach, forcing a groan from his lips. Heavier than a rat as well, with tiny limbs around a sallow, pear-shaped frame. Layers of amber-colored wings fluttered. If not for the brass nail it held over him, Lind might have smirked. "The dust of our kin. We want." Tiny, glittering eyes moved back and forth. "Our dust."

He felt cool air on his lower legs. The others must have ripped apart the sheets at the foot of the bed.

It repeated its demand, shrieking the last words and stomping a foot on a rib.

Pixies. The last he'd seen had been caged by Bluebottle the spriggan, a fence at his rag and bone shop. He ground them to powder, to glamour, and forced Tupp to collect from the Folk of London. Lind had once felt a sense of sympathy to Tupp for being under the spriggan's control. Released when Lind and Tupp robbed him, the pixies had swarmed over the spriggan. A horrible but deserved end. But it would have been wasteful to leave behind the milled glamour, so Lind took bags of the stuff.

Lind never imagined pixies would come looking for the glamour. How'd they find him?

Something sharp dragged across the soles of his feet and he screamed.

"Rings on his fingers, bells on his toes, he shall have trouble wherever he goes," sang the unseen pixies, who stank like split casks of last year's cider.

The bindings bit through the sheets, shirt and skin when he thrashed. Several snapped before the pixie atop him could stab down with the nail.

He struck the pixie, its middle giving way to his fist as if he had crushed a rotten apple. Its scream was shrill and awful.

The others flew to the window, breaking glass, or to the door, sending it slamming against the wall. More plaster fell.

Blood streaked the sheets, most his own. He plucked a wing from the dead pixie. With the warmth of his touch, it gleamed as if a scrap of gold leaf. He ripped the rest free of the corpse. Tupp wouldn't approve, but why trouble his partner's morals by confessing?

He hobbled to the center of the room. The floorboards had been pried apart, revealing where he had hidden his share of the remaining glamour. The pixies would have stolen away with it if not for the heavy chain he'd wrapped around the small bag. Lind didn't care why none of the Folk could stand the touch of iron. The thick links would have charred a pixie's hands to cinders.

He'd have to abandon the room, the building as well. If the pixies didn't return, something else would come calling, something nastier.

Lind ripped the sheets apart and wrapped the cleanest strips around his bloody legs. He then took everything of worth. The pixies had so thoroughly knotted the sleeves of his second, better shirt that he'd never be able to wear it again. He kept it for entry to the Exchange. As he dropped the worn file and chisel into the small sack he brought along when calling upon a houses, a strange sense of awareness filled him. He was looting his own room, and the haul wasn't worth more than a fourpenny except for what the Folk had brought: glamour, wings and ring. Suddenly fearful that the pixies had robbed him after all, he went to his pockets. But no, he found the ring where he'd left it and laughed. The Folk weren't so clever after all.

The makeshift bandages allowed him to make the long walk to Houndsditch. Countless restless voices, each seeking to capture passersby, rose from the Old Clothes Exchange. Lind breathed through his mouth to escape the varied stink of sweat-soaked clothes, of moldy clothes, and worthless clothes and, underneath the lot, the most wretched rags. But deeper into the Exchange, there'd be worse. His stomach murmured and churned at the memory of hare skins hanging raw, sold close to fatty cakes, the crusts brilliant with grease.

The hour was the busiest for the Exchange, and Lind stood next to the old-clothes men in their uniforms of tight gabardine coats and smocks, armed with fistfuls of stacked hats and shouldering sacks. Each tugged at their beards as they eyed their fellows, their rivals in line beside them. "Solomon never judged so much," Kapel would often tell Lind.

Yet Lind felt so comfortable among them. Did the Sight allow him to peer past their stern faces and thick gabardine? He saw men who acted as brothers when

they shared laughter and sips of plum brandy after a deal, white-bearded grand-fathers nodding praise over the shoulders of reading children, their language loose from the confines of church to be welcome in the home.

Mr Barling had boasted to his clients that he considered his climbing boys "me own brood, such li'l dears." But Lind remembered the sound of Barling's footsteps as he left his dears alone in the cramped basement, so dark, often so cold. The gonuphs had promised to be brothers. More like that Cain bloke. The underworld of London was no better or worse than these earlier families: kind when the rounds were brought and cruel when the finger comes down.

He sold to the Jew beside him his knotted shirt for a penny. Lind reached the gates and their toll-man, Barney Aaron, round of head and belly, held out a hand for a copper. His young son, already thick in the middle and with dull eyes, held a leather satchel that by the day's end would be so heavy it crept near the ground and would tempt any villain in London who guessed its contents.

Oh, he hated how that satchel taunted him. Lind paced some evenings in the company of a gin bottle and devised seven different schemes, including one that required a slavering mutt as a distraction. But once he stole from the Jews, he'd never be able to return to Kapel, so he would arrive at the Exchange early, when the young Aaron hefted a light satchel high over his shoulder.

As he pushed and slipped his way through the narrow paths of the Exchange, fingers tugged at his sack. He ignored the calls around him.

Atop a small stage in the center of the maze, Kapel stirred a kettle over a small stove and shouted through his smoke-colored beard, "Hot wine. Ha'penny a glass."

Lind winced at how clumsy his wrapped legs took the stage's steps. "Two glasses."

He dropped his sack to the wooden boards.

"It's good wine." Kapel poured from the ladle.

Lind acknowledged the lie with a nod. Kapel's insistence that every deal be made with the blessing of God remained amusing. So the old Jew had taught him a prayer over the acrid wine he sold.

"*Baruch atah —*"

A short figure roaming the Exchange caught his attention. Stockier than Tupp and with a wide cap of green moss and long, drooping feathers. Passed right near the stage but it didn't raise its gnarled head at him.

Lind began the prayer again, "*Baruch atah Adonai —*" but then that one of the Folk started a loud dicker over the torn sleeves of a coachman's coat atop one mound of clothes. The attendant Jew argued and showed the lining.

He heard Kapel clear his throat, so he muttered the middle part before finishing. "*Borey pahree hagoffem.*"

"Is good you are so eager, eh?" Kapel winked as he sipped. The wiry hair around Kapel's mouth was darker than the rest of the beard and made his teeth look large. "Will I have to turn out my pockets today?"Lind nodded but kept his eye on the irksome Folk who dropped broken eggshells into the palm of the Jew, who seemed pleased with himself. Poor bloke.Lind took the ring from his pocket and swallowed the wine, tepid and the more sour for it. He switched hands returning the glass to Kapel, and his fives dropped the ring into the red dregs left at the bottom.

When Kapel set the glass down with the others, the ring had been palmed, then cleaned with some spilt wine.

"A commendable piece," Kapel said softly. "I can give a good price."

Lind pantomimed searching through his sack as he spoke. "I need a very good price, my friend." He would give all the coins to trusting Tupp. Even if it meant Lind went hungry for a few days.

"Nu, don't I offer the best? You are either visiting better people to bring such finds. Or worse."

Lind nodded. "I fear it's both." His legs pained him. He thought of the walk to meet Tupp at the bridge. And then? Another job, more of the Folk, who hated him. Perhaps he should take the coin and leave London for good, escape the Folk. But the idea left him cold. Lonesome and cold.

"I'm up the flue."

"Oh?"

Lind nodded. The words wanted to rush out and he bit most down. Even weak wine on an empty stomach could make him foolish. He didn't dare talk of the Folk to Kapel. He might be wise, but Kapel would see him mad. Lind had to talk clever for once.

He whispered. "Worse than the traps, worse than a tuck up fair and watching your mates do the drop." Lind tugged at his collar to emulate being hanged.

"Tell me."

"I've made some...well, goods of a sort. There are folk who pay well for them. That ring there, the sorts of loot I've brought you, all came from them. But they're a queer lot and some aren't willing to buy. They'd rather take. And I don't think they care how they leave me."

"What are you selling, *boytchik*?"

"That I can't tell — "

"Then how can I help you?"

Lind stood there, not sure what to say. He didn't have an answer. There might not be one. He felt trapped by his heart.

"Stealing is no life. Listen to me. What I do is a little sin. You're a little sin to me as well, but one I enjoy helping." Kapel climbed down the stage and motioned for Lind to follow. "I would be sorry if you would be found dead in some alley."

Lind thought of Eur Du's threat and shuddered. He followed Kapel through the Exchange and watched as the old Jew took his time greeting merchants, arguing over a price, until they reached the gates.

Kapel then turned to him and pressed some folded pound notes into Lind's palm. Lind, displeased that the advice would benefit a bumpkin squire from the countryside and not a dedicated cracksman who knew the streets, the housetops since he was a child, made a show of counting the pounds.

"More than enough for the ring, I think. And for you to leave."

Lind hugged Kapel before leaving the Exchange. Perhaps for the last time.

ON THE WAY TO WATERLOO BRIDGE, LIND stopped at a whelk-seller. Half his cart sold for a penny four of the large, pickled snails on chipped saucers, the other offered them live in a tub of cold, scummy water. A little girl shivered beneath a tattered shawl, the ends trailing into the brine and the weight of lead, as she wiped the whelk shells to a shine. Lind bought four from the man. Though bitter, the flesh was firm and would last in his stomach. He wiped his lips, then held out a penny to the girl, who had cautious eyes but quick fingers. Lind regretted that the penny would end up in the man's pocket by the night's end.

The bridge's toll-man barely glanced at Lind when he approached the turnstile. "Ha'penny to cross." The man shifted on his seat and the sound of a bottle rolling about his feet made the man blush and cough. Lind joined the other furtive folk who dared walk the bridge on a barren night. Half were desperate, the other half not to be trusted, which made Lind smirk and wonder to which he belonged.

Lind often found Tupp sitting, or once lying, atop some ledge with his gaze on the west, following the setting sun.

He saw Tupp standing on the stone edge now, still as a statue, yet a moment of worry stole through Lind. A simple step forward would topple Tupp. Waterloo earned its second name of Bridge of Sighs after women had taken to leaping off it into the Thames. Lind looked over the edge. No boats in the cold water, so perhaps no one else had seen him. Pub talk had said the boats carried bible and coin for anyone dragged alive from the waters. Redemption of soul and pocket.

Lind advanced stealthily, partially due to his sore legs, but also because this was one of the few times he could observe a wistful expression on Tupp.

At first, Lind thought the Folk could only feel anger or delight; they seemed to only raise their voices in rage or cheer. As if children, awful children, had magic behind their whims and with no thought for anyone but themselves.

But in the past month, Lind had glimpsed moments beyond growl and grin. The way Tupp watched him with such interest. Treating any of the Folk as if they were men of London was dangerous. He worried he'd let his guard down and end up like that poor sod who embraced Jenny last night.

Yet, when Lind had stepped close enough to see the wistful expression on Tupp's face, see how the wind made Tupp's blue eyes water, Lind felt reluctance to think that his partner ever meant him harm.

Tupp glanced down at Lind, then gestured for Lind to join him on the ledge.

Why didn't the gusts carry off his askew top hat? Lind didn't want to test his scratched legs against the wind. And Tupp had never made such a request of him before when they met.

"Only one step up. Perhaps two. You are a master cracksman..."

Lind sighed. He cautiously climbed up on the ledge. The wind snatched at his coat. He felt it tug him back and forth, then, as if it had decided the water would be a better fate than the stone of the bridge, the wind howled and pulled him down.

Tupp grabbed Lind before he fell.

"You're limping. You're hurt."

Lind sat down. "Oh, some pests came looking for our haul." He reached into his coat and withdrew first the pouches of glamour and then a handful of coins. "Your share."

"Sizable. Have you ever been to Wessex?"

"No."

"I come from there. And there are days I miss it so much that not even glamour can keep me from feeling sick." He shook the coins. "This could pay for both of us to travel there."

"And what would we do when the glamour runs out?"

"There are fewer Folk there. Less iron, too. But we won't be taking this," Tupp said as he held the glamour out over the water."

"What? No, that's worth a fortune!" Lind reached out until he risked slipping from the bridge.

"True. But some fortunes aren't measured in coin. But years." Tupp opened his hand and the bags splashed into the noisome river below.

He pointed out movement below. Jenny's head broke the water's surface, long and limp hair hiding much of her face.

Lind stiffened next to Tupp.

"Your debt is paid, mortal," she said, her voice melodic despite being full of the Thames. "And my silence bought as well, when kith and kin ask where you have gone." Then she sank, as if eager to walk the cold river bottom.

Tupp realized Lind clenched his hand tight. "Fewer Folk in Wessex?" he asked.

Tupp nodded and smiled. "If you wish, you need only be bothered by one." Tupp leaned in close. The feel of soft lips overcame the rough stone upon which they sat. The heat of the kiss kept at bay the icy wind.

Lind then whispered in Tupp's ear, "And how would we live?"

"I promise 'with great mischief.'"

Worse than Alligators

LATER, JAMESON WISHED HE WOULD RE-
member that night for the twenty minutes spent arm-in-arm with Eddie, walking Grubb through the neighborhood. Those minutes had everything: chill,
autumn air that captured their breath in little puffs; the warmth of a boyfriend
pressing against you, sometimes bumping into you when one of you misjudged
your next step; a dog's curlicue tail wagging, the equivalent to a wide grin. Perfect. Tranquil. Even the moon was bright, as if the cosmos wanted to say, "Be
happy, Jameson."

Eddie happened to be a talker. Silence = worry, so he would break the quiet
every now and then. But Jameson didn't mind. Being chatty wasn't a fault. His
boyfriend had no faults.

If they could just keep walking, mile after mile, until they found themselves
directly under that glowing moon and see everything bathed in its romantic
light, Jameson would be content. Content at seventeen. That was some sort of
oxymoronic thought, but as he shivered at the cold and Eddie leaned into him
more to share his warmth, even the impossible seemed so likely.

"Do you think they burnt the house down?" Eddie asked.

Jameson shook his head. "Sis was warned, on pain of lights out at eight, not to touch the stove, oven, not even the toaster."

"If we didn't have to go back...if we could just stay out..."

"You're mind reading now." Jameson kissed Eddie's forehead. Well, actually his long bangs, since it was an awkward and sudden kiss, but it made Eddie smile. "There will be other nights like this."

"Babysitting is not as awful as I imagined."

"Babysitting is one or two. Seven ten year olds is chaperoning. Better pay. But I may fall asleep before they do. You'll have to poke me, keep me awake."

"I promise."

They had circled back to his street. Jameson wanted to stop right there, in the middle of the quiet neighborhood, and make out with Eddie for just a while; the unspoken agreement with Jameson's parents had been Eddie could come over and help oversee Madeline's sleep-over but there'd be no kiss-and-tell.

But Grubb began growling. Low, and reverberating, as if the growl got caught in the shar-pei's many neck folds before being released. Both boys began looking around.

"What's that?" Eddie asked. He was staring at the corner. Jameson saw nothing odd. Only the standard neighborhood hedges. A lamppost.

Eddie slipped his arm out from under Jameson's own. He crouched a little, as if he was going to ask Grubb what was making the dog so edgy, but he only pointed down, toward the far curb. "See?"

Something pale was caught in the storm drain. Every autumn, the neighborhood's drains became clogged with detritus of fallen leaves and twigs. As a kid, Jameson had felt it was his civic duty on the walk to and from school to kick clear the grates — his duty until it became incredibly boring, which it always did by the third one.

Whatever it was looked small and thin but as white as the moon above, even stealing some of its luminescence. Maybe mushrooms? White slender mushrooms? Could they even grow on layers of autumn muck?

Eddie went to take a closer look, and Grubb lunged, not at him but in the direction of the grate. The swift tug almost pulled the leash from Jameson's grasp. When Grubb realized he was not going to follow after Eddie, the barking began.

Jameson shushed Grubb and gently tugged on the dog's collar with one hand as they both watched Eddie stop just inches shy of the drain.

Eddie shuddered and backpedaled and whatever the wriggling white things were, they stretched in his direction a moment before Eddie stomped on the grate. It would have been comical, should have been, but Eddie looked more afraid than disgusted.

"What did you see? Nightcrawlers?"

Jameson put his arm around his boyfriend, who looked pale and shaken.

"My worst day at elementary school," Jameson said. "No matter how much your dad insists, a jar of worms is not a good show-and-tell. The nicknames I had to endure."

Eddie reached down to pet Grubb's velour fur. The dog whined at first but once he saw they were headed back home, his tail began to sway again.

As Jameson slipped his house keys from his coat pocket, Eddie watched their backs. "What is wrong with you?" Jameson asked.

"Think your folks would know if I snuck into the liquor cabinet?"

"Not funny. Madeline would then ask if the girls could have a sip of whatever you were drinking. And that would lead to cataclysmic grounding." He turned a key in the deadbolt. "So, unless you feel like going to prom stag — "

"Open the door."

The girls, led by his sister, came running. Grubb eagerly met them, and was soon being petted and rubbed and pulled by half the bevy.

"Can we make no'mores?" Madeline asked. She clutched a jar to her chest, but Jameson couldn't see the label. Rose-colored glitter covered some of her forehead and cheeks.

"No'mores?"

Madeline rolled her eyes, as if her brother had absolutely no understanding of anything. "Better than s'mores. You don't need a campfire. It's toast spread with melted marshmallows — you melt them in the microwave — and then this." She held out a jar of Nutella. The lid looked very loose, and Jameson suspected that half the jar had already been devoured.

"Sure."

In the kitchen, the girls had already made a mess without using anything with a heating element. Eddie sang Red Caps songs off-tune as he helped clear the center island and Jameson plugged in the toaster.

He fed it the first slices and was looking for the bag of marshmallows in the cupboard pantry when he felt a little tug at his sleeve.

One of the girls. She was a bit heavier than the rest. And her mother had permitted a terrible haircut that only made her face rounder. Jameson tried to remember her name: either Chloe or Zoey.

"Hmm?"

"Can I use the bathroom?" A dollop of glitter on one round cheek looked like a mole.

He blinked. "Sure. You walked right past it — "

She shook her head. Her voiced dropped to a whisper. "No. A different one. Upstairs." She took a two-step to reinforce the idea she needed to go real bad real soon.

Jameson leaned down. "Oh. Yeah, it's at the top of the stairs. Our little secret, okay?"

The girl neither agreed nor thanked him, but dashed off.

Curious, Jameson walked into the downstairs bathroom. Yet again messy but unoccupied. Madeline and the girls must have been playing with the talcum powder because a fine dusting covered parts of the sink and some of the mirror, though much had been wiped clear. He lifted up the toilet seat, prepared for the worst, but there was nothing sick there other than blue water.

Eddie was picking up toast, dropping it on to plates and blowing on his singed fingertips. He looked calm and Jameson decided not to pursue whatever had shaken him outside. It could have been a dead squirrel. Eddie donated birthday money to animal shelters. Yeah, a dead critter, maybe even a possum, would have freaked him out.

It took longer than Jameson expected, but finally, balancing seven plates on arms and hands, they brought into the den of eager girls the no'mores. Madeline was reading from a book and the rest were circling her. All except Chloe, who sat next to the couch on the floor a bit apart from the others. The sight made Jameson wince. Why was the heavyset girl always the outsider? He would have to pull Madeline aside and tell her that a proper hostess makes sure all her guests are entertained.

The no'mores disappeared into sweet-tooth filled mouths. Crumbs stuck to small chins. "We need milk," Eddie faux-shouted, as if calling out for water for a fire, and he dashed off to the kitchen, making the girls laugh and redouble when he brought back the carton.

"Open your mouths and each gets a pour."

Jameson gave Eddie first a raised eyebrow, then a little stink-eye.

"What...I promise not to miss." And he didn't, each girl lining up to have a little milk poured into her open mouth. A couple wanted seconds, but Eddie refused until every one had firsts.

"What are you reading?" Jameson asked Madeline. The paperback looked ready to crumble apart, the pages the same yellow as old newspapers in the garage from last spring that had yet to be recycled.

Madeline lifted the book up to show the cover. *Occult for the Parlour.*

"What's a parlour?" one of the girls asked.

"It's where Colonel Mustard shot someone," Eddie said.

"Zoey brought it."

"My father has a lot of books." She blushed at the attention.

"You must live in a library," Madeline said. "And sleep on a shelf."

"Be nice." Jameson realized the finger he raised was the exact same gesture his parents used.

Madeline returned her attention to the book, turning pages, before becoming animated once more. "Oooh, can we hypnotize you, Eddie?"

"Wait — what?" he asked.

Jameson took the book from Madeline. A page tore loose and fluttered to her lap. He looked at the chapter "Entertaining with Hypnotism." The black-and-white illustration showed a thickly coifed man with raised hands that shot tiny lightning bolts at a wide-eyed woman dressed like a prude.

The girls began to call out, demanding Eddie sit down and let himself by hypnotized, though several of them mispronounced the word, adding new consonants.

Jameson looked over at Eddie, who shrugged and wore a half-grin. Then he turned back to the book and thumbed through the pages, skimming the various "lessons."

"Please?" Madeline made the single word last almost half a minute.

"It's up to him."

She turned and looked up at Eddie and held her hands clasped in mock-begging.

"Okay. But don't make me do anything stupid. And no one takes any pictures or videos. I don't want to find a Vine of me acting like a monkey."

The girls laughed. Jameson noticed that even Zoey seemed less anxious.

Madeline guided Eddie to sit next to her and then snapped her fingers at Jameson so he would hand back the book. She began reading and providing Eddie instructions on how to relax, to close his eyes, to count backwards. She shushed the other girls, who were chattering about what they wanted Eddie to do once he was "under."

Jameson tidied the room a bit but really watched. Eddie was being a good sport and listening to everything Madeline told him to do.

At one point he made a loud snoring sound that caused a ripple of laughter in his audience. Madeline smacked his chest with the book and chided him not to fake. She had him start counting backwards from one hundred. His voice grew softer as he passed the seventies until his mouth barely moved and no one could hear the count.

"You're deep asleep but you can still hear me, right?"

Eddie dipped his head a fraction.

Red Caps

"Eddie," Madeline said, "tell me your full name."

"Edmund Mitchell Standiford." His voice sounded distant. Jameson decided he must recommend Eddie try out for the school play next time.

"How old are you?"

"Seventeen."

"I want you to try and lift your left..." Madeline glanced at a page in the book, "lift your left arm. But it's heavy. Too heavy. Like it's made of lead."

Jameson watched as Eddie did seem to struggle to lift his arm from where it rested on the sofa cushion.

Grubb whined. Madeline shushed the dog.

"This is boring stuff." She turned a few pages. Eddie still sought to raise his arm, which trembled. Madeline shut the book. "So, Eddie, you have to listen to my command." She leaned down to whisper to the nearest girls. Her eyes went to look at Jameson.

"You have to kiss me. You have to kiss all of us."

"Whoah," Jameson said and put a firm hand on Madeline's shoulder, keeping her from moving closer to his boyfriend. "No kissing."

A pouting chorus of whines and boos.

"What can we do then?"

Jameson sat down on the arm of the sofa. "Eddie, why don't you tell them what you saw in the storm drain." Nothing like talk about worms to send the girls squealing.

"Fingers. A little girl's fingers." Eddie's face looked pained. "Wet hair and her squirming fingers." He stood up and screamed.

The circle of girls erupted, echoing his cry as they backed away. Grubb began barking.

Jameson grabbed hold of Eddie, who shut his mouth and blinked as if he really had come out of a trance. Eddie wrapped his arms around Jameson and shuddered as if trying to bring up a sob.

"You're scaring everyone," he said softly to Eddie. He thought Eddie whispered back, "She was horrible," but he couldn't mean Madeline. Bratty on occasion was her worst.

Grubb's barking became the most annoying thing in the room, and despite Madeline's hold on his neck, he rushed off in the direction of the bathroom. When Jameson turned around to tell the girls to stay put, he saw they had clustered together.

With Eddie, he followed the snarling and scratching sounds to find Grubb half in the shower stall, his head shaking back and forth, something white in his jaws. Jameson knelt down and saw it vaguely looked like a long glove but had the texture of the melted marshmallow used in the no'mores. One of the girls must have dropped her treat, maybe even a few uncooked marshmallows, and Grubb had begun munching. The dog whined when Jameson took hold of the gooey mess by one wet and cold edge. It pulled almost apart. He dropped it into the toilet and flushed. The end that resembled fingers wiggled as it went down the drain. Grubb whined and kept returning to sniff the drain in the stall. It barked once, twice at it.

"Both of you," Jameson said, "need to stop with the scares." He wiped his hands with a fresh towel.

The girls didn't like hearing that it was lights-out time. Amid the whines came Madeline's plea with the book. "But there's more — "

Eddie stole it from her grasp. "A good magician knows when to end the show."

"A movie at least."

"You watched two already. Bedtime." Jameson turned to Eddie. "Help me get all the blankets."

Together, they helped rearrange the living room for maximum sleeping occupancy with pillows and sleeping bags, and then had to redo it once more because Madeline didn't like it that this girl was sleeping so close to her when she wanted a different BFF on her right.

Grubb lay protectively amongst them.

Jameson turned out the light. He led Eddie into the small den with the desk that was more of a workbench where his father would stay up late making ornate fishing lures that had names like garage bands. Orange Craw. Thunder Bug. They decorated cubbyholes along the walls beside mounted bass and salmon. When he was seven, Jameson had snuck into the den one morning to play with the colorful lures. More than a decade had passed, as well as several awkward attempts and father-son fishing trips, and still Jameson associated his father's hobby with the memory of hooks catching in the flesh of his palm and a tetanus shot. He eyed the lures now warily. But the den was closer to the living room. He could keep an ear trained for the girls, who peppered the darkness with whispers and giggles.

Eddie collapsed in a beat-up recliner, the only other chair in the room, and opened up the book.

Jameson swiveled to face him. "Do you think I'm boring?"

"No." Eddie laughed the word into multiple syllables.

"It's just that...I don't know. When I was Madeline's age, I didn't have sleepovers. Or invented treats..." He shook his head. "No'mores?"

Red Caps

Eddie rolled his eyes with the same precision as Jameson's little sister, which stung rather than comforted. Eddie was more like her than him. They both were barely contained vessels of chaos, so quick to say something, anything, rarely sitting still. Eddie already had shifted in the recliner as if unable to relax.

"I wasn't asking boys to kiss me at that age either." Jameson suspected that Eddie had kissed a boy first. He knew stuff. Stuff that made Jameson both thrilled and worried that Eddie would grow bored of him one day.

"You can have one now."

Flirting. Eddie was a brilliant flirter. How does someone learn that?

"Relax. I only want to kiss you."

"That was some performance. I mean your screaming."

Eddie paled. "Yeah. I just...I mean, none of this" — he lifted the book — "is real. I planned on snoring when it became boring. But when you asked me about the grate — "

"So, wait, that horror show..."

He shrugged "I *thought* I saw...someone down the drain. A little girl reaching up, fingers through the grate as if she wanted me to pull her up. Or pull me down."

"You probably saw a kid's doll that got washed down the gutter and stuck there."

Eddie threw the book at Jameson. "This stuff is all too creepy."

"Isn't that one of the rules to having a sleepover? Have a séance or something?"

Eddie stood and stretched, noticed Jameson staring at his exposed briefs that rose above his blue jeans, and smirked. He then took the few steps to cross the room and lean down, resting a hand on each of the desk chair's arms and trapping Jameson.

"Didn't I mention a liquor cabinet?" he whispered while bringing his face close to Jameson's. "That is what I think a sleepover needs."

Flustered, Jameson lost the gift of language for several seconds. Which made Eddie laugh, loud for a moment until he cupped a hand over his own mouth, trapping the remainder of the laugh behind a smile.

"We can't."

"I know. I am gonna see if there's any Nutella left, though." Eddie stopped in the doorway. He gestured toward the living room.

Jameson didn't understand until he heard. Nothing. They must have fallen asleep.

Eddie gave him a thumbs-up and headed for the kitchen..

Red Caps

Jameson sighed. He realized he'd always be the boy his parents could trust. "Opposites attract" had to have some truth.

He flipped the book's pages, wincing in his head at what he found: black-and-white photographs of people with their lips stretched wide and weird balloons coming out of their mouths. He read the caption about mediums vomiting ectoplasm, white stuff that was supposed to be from the spirit world. He thought of that gunk Grubb had been chewing. He didn't like the thought it might have been something...eerie.

A timid knock startled Jameson. He almost fell out of the chair turning to the open doorway to see Zoey standing there sniffing. The distinct stink of piss came to him.

"Aww, what's wrong, hon?" he said as he walked over. "Did you...did you have an accident?"

"N-no...I-I." She wiped her face and looked back toward the living room. "They haven't come back yet. I didn't want to go, I told them so. And when Madeline c-called me a baby I got scared and angry and I peed. I hid in the blankets and they all went and now they haven't come back."

"What? Went where?"

"To look for Carmen Winstead."

Eddie appeared, licking chocolate from his fingertips. "What's wrong?"

Jameson shook his head. "Who's Carmen?" He guided Zoey back toward the living room. The bottom half of the girl's pajamas was soaked with urine. He saw that Grubb stood beside the front door. The dog glanced at him, then whined and pawed at the wood.

Zoey trembled. "She's...she's a girl who got bullied at some school near here. And the kids tossed her down the storm drain and she died and her ghost...her ghost came and took the bullies one by one. And you can see her... you can see she writes a warning if you go into the bathroom and spray the mirror with powder and say her name three times."

Jameson remembered the talcum powder spilled in the bathroom.

"And after Eddie, what you guys talked about under hyp-hypnosis. Madeline waited until she thought you were both asleep and she dared all of us to go to the storm drain at the end of the block. But I didn't want to."

"Fuck." Jameson could just imagine a half-dozen ten-year-old girls, dressed only in pajamas, standing around a corner late at night. It was a child abductor's smorgasbord. He scrambled on his coat. Eddie did the same, but Jameson told him to take Zoey into the bathroom. When she started to wail and begged not to go to the downstairs bathroom, he told Eddie to take her upstairs and clean her up.

Red Caps

Grubb pawed, more agitated, and barked. He slipped right past Jameson's legs when the door opened and dashed toward the end of the block. Jameson ran after Grubb, but he could see as he dashed off the front porch there was no cluster of girls arranged around the storm drain. Only a barking dog.

He almost began shouting their names, but hesitated raising his voice and disturbing the neighbors. Behind him, he heard Eddie's voice, calling out for Madeline and the others. A trickle of anger flushed through Jameson's blood with the current of fear. Why wouldn't Eddie do as he was told?

Jameson looked around the hedges, hoping, readying himself for the girls to leap out and yell "Boo." But no, at the corner, there was just Grubb. And Eddie standing there, staring down.

"Help me," Jameson said. And fell to his knees besides the grate. Eddie took his cell phone out, was dialing the police. By the phone's weak light, Jameson glimpsed a pale figure down in the storm drain slipping away, leaving behind the distant sobbing of girls, or was that his own? He thought he heard over the sobs a little girl laugh.

Only Lost Boys Are Found

You're surprisingly normal despite having grown up in a house with an extreme quantity of closets. Every room has at least one. At the top of the steps is a linen closet. Your parents' room has two, a his and hers. Your sister, older and more adventurous, had chosen the other bedroom with two. You don't mind having just a single closet; what good are closets, really? Too shallow, too small. When closed, a closet is like looking at a wall featuring a doorknob. Weird. These days people have chests of drawers to put away clothes. And what guy your age hangs up his shirts or jeans? You sometimes sniff your clothes to see if you can get another day out of them.

Your Closet

What you keep in your closet, in no order suggesting proximity or stratum:

A dog-eared paperback, assigned for freshman English class.

Your teacher is convinced that every great work of Literature (stress the capital "L") can be turned inside out to reveal a fairy tale. You haven't read much more than the first few pages of the book, bought at a flea market so it's maimed, without a cover.

Something about a boy with a flashlight who is climbing down stairs. Or maybe it's a mountain, or stairs set on the side of a mountain. But the boy is scared that his flashlight will die before he reaches the bottom.

A broken iPod, screen cracked in a cool pattern after you dropped it in the school parking lot and fucking Adrian Jesson drove over it. You don't think it was an accident.

A pile that is actually a moss-green corduroy jacket you found at the same flea market as the book and thought might look cool if you ever had the need for a ritzy jacket. Only it's too big and smells...well, mossy.

A shoebox of mixed Lego minifigs — ninjas and pirates mostly — that used to belong to Neil Jesson (yes, younger brother to the aforementioned Adrian). You started playing together in third grade. Neil always wanted Hollywood to make a movie where Blackbeard invaded Japan.

A wrapped square box, the dust hiding the shine of the metallic gold paper. A Valentine's Day present for Neil. But he never showed up at school that day. Or the day after or the one after that. You don't remember what the gift is but tearing off the ribbon and the wrapping paper would be something awful, a felony of love, so you keep it way in the back of the closet so as not to glimpse the box too often. You miss Neil.

One thing definitely not in the closet: you. When you turned ten (August, it was brutally hot) you told your parents that inviting girls from school for your birthday party was just okay but you were much more interested in which boys showed. And they knew then the truth, and not too much later they had a talk with you so you'd be sure of the truth as well. And they were fine with you.

But not everyone is so lucky. You know this. When Neil never showed, you texted him — at first gentle concerns, then frantic worries. No replies. You dialed and left messages. Nothing. You even called Neil's home wanting to know what happened. Adrian answered both times, the last cursing you out before hanging up. His harsh voice left you feeling like crumpled paper. You are convinced that they somehow found out about you and him and sent him off someplace far away. Maybe to an asylum or boarding school. You feel guilty — you should have been more careful, kept your affection quiet. You should not have urged he come out. Neil was always so shy. You remember how he kissed with his eyes closed and then kept them shut for a few seconds afterward, as if he was afraid to look at you. And you were the one who always began the kiss. Yeah, you feel guilty.

The Refrigerator
YOU SUPPOSE THE FRIDGE IS SORT OF LIKE

a closet, only cold, icy in spots, and thrumming with electricity. No really, it is "like closet" — there are even forgotten things at the very back. A jar once for pickles but now holding the remains of a hollandaise sauce made last year. A roll of film from when your sister wanted to be a famous photographer. Yogurt that is no longer alive.

You grab an armful of butter and eggs and bacon and head over to the stove. You leave the fridge door open just in case you need something else.

Neil taught you how to make your favorite breakfast right. He stayed over one night before either of you had decided you were *more* than friends. Your mother always cooked eggs in the pan and bacon in the microwave. But Neil woke a few minutes earlier than you and was already at the stove when you climbed downstairs. His hair was seriously stuck in bedhead mode. But you didn't tease him; calling attention to that would leave Neil silent and withdrawn all afternoon.

He made the most incredible eggs and bacon. And you devoured the plate he made you and insisted right then and there he repeat himself so you could watch and learn. And instead of refusing or complaining, he just smiled and did so. And yes, you wanted to kiss him — the first time you ever felt that way.

Raw bacon goes into the skillet first. Let it bubble and warp as it cooks. Watch out for the fireworks of launched hot grease.

When it's shriveled down to crisp strips, ruddy meat and amber fat that all taste of 100% salty nitrite goodness, you lift them onto a plate. Then crack the eggs into the same pan, making two yellow eyes staring back at you, the whites turning brown and black at the edges from the hot bacon grease. And you start shaving fine bits of butter down onto the whites, followed with a dusting of pepper. The eyes will bubble and become jaundiced but they will soon be the best ever eggs imaginable.

Just as you're bringing your plate to the table, you wish, for the thousandth time, that Neil was sitting across from you with a subtle, pleased expression at teaching you so well.

Third-Floor Boys' Bathroom
DID YOU KNOW AN OLD-FASHIONED TERM

for bathroom is water closet?

You're heading to the cafeteria when someone grabs you by the collar from behind and shoves you into the bathroom. In the mirrors on one wall you catch a glimpse of Adrian's squared and ruddy face before he pushes you into an open stall. The door slams back and catches shut.

You back up until you are against the toilet. The paper dispenser is empty, broken, and covered in coarse graffiti. You doubt a girl would ever want to do the things someone wrote.

"Listen. I don't have time to repeat this," you hear Adrian say. "And I don't even know if I'm doing right...but maybe you can help him."

You go even more tense at *him*. *Him*. *Neil*. "Where is he?" you ask.

Adrian's sneakers are both untied, the laces no longer anywhere near white. "I think...I think he's scared and hiding."

You repeat the question, noting the irony that you are a bit scared right now.

"I said some things. I didn't mean to — big brothers tease. We're supposed to, but I think I went too far — "

You hear the bathroom door open and you hear Adrian say, "Get the fuck out of here," followed by the sound of running away.

"I've heard him crying. I'll be in my room and I'll hear him, but when I cross the hall and open his door — nothing. No one's there. I've gone through his whole room, looked under the bed, everything. But the crying doesn't stop and I can't find him."

You think this is the cruelest thing Adrian could ever say to you.

"I can't help him. But maybe you can. And you have to. I can't take it anymore, hearing him cry and not being able to stop it."

You refuse to say anything and finally you watch Adrian's dirty sneakers move out of sight and hear the bathroom door open. He's gone. You sit down on the toilet and rub the sides of your head and wonder why love and siblings are just so awful.

Your Closet
WHAT DO YOU HAVE THAT WOULD HELP

with a rescue mission?

It's Saturday morning and you're groggy because you couldn't sleep last night because of what Adrian told you yesterday. It's crazy, but, as you lie half in, half out of your closet, with the Legos in reach and the gift within sight, you're willing to believe.

Because Saturdays are magical for kids, have been ever since the first morning cartoon was shown on television. At fifteen you hope there's still enough of a kid in you to find Neil with Saturday's help.

Your Sister's Closets

She keeps things needed for adven-

ture.

She's still asleep. Does so till after twelve or even one on the weekends. So you twist the doorknob oh so quietly, oh so cautiously. There's more at risk than a pillow thrown at your head. Such a territorial incursion might get you grounded, and you need your entire Saturday to stage the rescue of the boy you love.

Her room smells...well, weird. A bit of pine from whatever gear she takes to camp at the Barrens, the funk from nearly a dozen sneakers, brine ghosts from found shells that should have been better cleaned.

You glance at her lying in bed. Still in jeans and a sweatshirt.

The window open, letting in cool air. She must have snuck back in through the window from whatever exploits she's now sleeping off. So step by step you make your way to the first closet, partially open.

Your Sister's Closets — No. 1

Ugh, clothes and clothes and more

clothes. Doesn't she own something other than sweats and Lycra? Not to mention more stinking footwear. Aren't girls supposed to have toes that smell like sugar cookies or something? Not like...wet schnauzer.

Your Sister's Closets — No. 2

Shut. At least the doors slide along

a track. You worry about a creak, but the left side moves as if freshly greased. Inside is the stuff that would make every extreme athlete, every stunt double to Indiana Jones, drool. Scuba gear. A pile of rope and pitons. An actual grappling hook. A helmet and chest pads. A lacrosse stick. Three different backpacks.

Your fingers are just closing around the molded plastic grip to the nearest backpack when you hear "Stop. Right. There."

You look over your shoulder. She's sitting up in bed. Worse, she's holding a lacrosse ball in one hand, tosses it up once for menacing effect. Her eyes are a bit crusted over with sleep, so her aim for your head might end up at crotch level, not only ruining your day but any chance of reunion celebration with Neil.

"What does that pinhead of yours imagine it's doing rifling through my gear?"

You think fast over your options. Truth? Nah, she'd mock you even if she did half believe you. You don't remember her once consoling you after Neil left. She was always out with her friends or on the phone. She never cared. Better to lie. "I need some stuff to get back at Adrian for what he did to me on Friday."

She grips the lacrosse ball hard. But you know by the thoughtful look on her face, by the emerging smile, you're in the clear. One, she likes the thought of revenge; two, she won't bother to ask for details because she doesn't care that much; three, she hates Adrian (rumors are that he tried to smack her ass as she walked through the hallway at school, further rumors of what happened next range from Adrian chipping a tooth from being shoved face-first into a water fountain to her pantsing him).

"Okay. Make it quick. Then get out."

You grab the backpack, look longingly at the grappling hook because it's so cool with the barbed flares, but decide that you'd only risk hurting yourself and possibly Neil if you did try to throw it. But you take the helmet and chest pads. The ball is thrown at her bedroom door just as you're leaving, huffing as you rush out with your hands full.

In the backpack is a heavy flashlight, a laminated but bent sheet identifying *Poisonous Lichens and Mosses of North America*, a couple of packets of instant coffee mix, a screwdriver, and even some wadded-up dollar bills among some loose papers at the bottom (probably her old homework).

In your room you choose your favorite T-shirt, the one with Harley Quinn from the Batman cartoon — the good one, the one you watched with Neil on DVD, not the recent crap — and say in a falsetto, "Right away, Mr. J," before you put on the helmet.

Your face quickly heats up.

As you ride your bike to Neil's house, you feel a bit like a knight in modern armor. A knight on a quest to save his prince.

The Jessons' Basement Closet
Actually this looks more like a root

cellar. But you need to enter the house and find a way to Neil's bedroom. The driveway is empty, an oil stain on the cement marking where Adrian's pickup once sat.

You use the screwdriver to pry off the simple lock keeping the doors shut. Then out comes the flashlight. You descend the stairs. Much of the basement is utility-oriented: washer and dryer against one wall, rickety metal shelves hold-ing plastic totes of distant holiday decorations along another.

You hear a whisper calling to you. No, more of a hiss. You shine your light at the source: an old water heater that looks like the belly of a termite queen, rounded and immense, the many pipes rising off it like a child's drawing of how a centipede should walk. You take a step closer. You hear water dripping.

The circle of light slips past the pipes and cement walls to find a door hidden behind the water heater. It's small, swollen from the dampness so that the indi-vidual boards bulge and gap, and the metal hinges are rusty. You have to bend down to approach it.

The Secret Basement Closet

NO HANDLE ON THIS CLOSET, JUST A round hole where a doorknob should be. A dark hole, too wide to be a safe peep-hole. You nudge the door open with your foot. Thanks to the flashlight you see it's over a foot drop to some cement stairs coiling down and down.

A trip deep into Saturday-morning logic, but one that also reeks of damp things.

The stairwell is slippery and there's no handrail. As you descend, you count slow under the hot breath that fills the helm. By one hundred your feet splash in puddles on the steps, warm water that spills down each. After you've lost count at around three hundred and sixty-five or so, the water is up to your knees; you have the urge to pee.

Soon, you're wading through waist-deep water (and you did pee, several steps ago, because you could get away with it in the dark, but you'll never tell anyone that), your flashlight's beam waves back and forth over the water until it finds a figure approaching on a boat. No, a raft without sail. You wave and call out. Could it be Neil?

But no, as the raft approaches the stairwell you see it's not your boyfriend. For a moment, you think it's your sister, for the pirate has her features, down to the tiny scar below her lips from when she fell from the monkey bars as a toddler. But not her boobs, which were never really big anyway, which torments her no end. The bandanna she wraps about her neck when jogging hides much of the pirate's short hair. But the pirate is missing one eye. Your light catches move-ment in the empty socket: a tiny beak, shiny eyes, atop a bit of fluff. At that you gasp.

"So you're the one who's been lighting up the sky," the pirate says, nodding at your flashlight. "Thought the moon had come down below a while."

"What's wrong with your eye?"

"Polite boy, aren't you? If you ever been at sea you'd know that all apprentice pirates must raise their own parrots from a chick before they earn their peg." The pirate — the apprentice pirate, really — makes a soft, clicking sound and lifts an oyster cracker to her missing eye. The beak plucks the cracker in a second.

"Why are you here? It's not syrupy eel season for months," the apprentice pirate asks.

"Uh, no, I don't want any eels."

The Closet-Raft

YOU SHINE YOUR LIGHT ONTO THE RAFT

and see it's actually a massive closet door, the knob serving as the rudder.

"What's on the other side of the water?"

The apprentice pirate squints her remaining eye. "Danger. Not much else. Not really sure. Other than danger."

"Would you take me across?"

"You have coin of the realm?"

You root around in your sister's backpack for the cash you saw earlier. You pull out some of the papers. The apprentice pirate catches one before it falls into the water. "Eh, what's this?"

Only one side is blank. On the other is a black & white photo of Neil, a photocopy from his Facebook account, with the words *This boy is missing. We miss him. Have you seen him?* Below that is an e-mail with your sister's name.

You stare at the flier long enough for the apprentice pirate to clear her throat. You always thought your sister didn't give a shit about Neil. She had made fun of you finally meeting a guy in time for Valentine's. But the flyers...dozens of them. You imagine that when you thought she was out with her friends, she was handing them out to strangers on the street. When she was chatting on the phone, she was asking if anybody had seen Neil.

You fall to your knees on the closet-raft. "Damn." You owe her an apology for an accusation never voiced.

"So you're looking for him? Lost boys and pirates don't get along — "

"You're only an apprentice pirate."

"True that." She feeds the parrot chick another cracker. "How did you lose him?"

"I'm...I'm not sure."

"That will make finding him harder."

The Closet-Raft

Bobs along the strange lake. Every so often the apprentice pirate adjusts the rudder. You give her the few dollars you found in the backpack.

When your flashlight — dying, so you only dare turn it on for a minute or so every once in a while — catches sight of a dock, you feel relief.

"Here," the apprentice pirate says, handing you a glass canning jar. It's empty but for a tiny sliver, dark and moist at the bottom.

"It's my last bit of syrupy eel. You might find yourself hungry along the way."

As you hop on to the docks, you thank the apprentice pirate and wish her luck on her PSATs (Pirate Scoundrel Aptitude Test?) or whatever exams she needs to graduate to full peg leg and crossbones.

A flagstone path emerges from the dock. You follow it through the dark, your eyes struggling to see any detail more than a few inches away.

You risk draining the flashlight, now a flickering beam. The glint of metal ahead catches your attention.

A ninja, all dressed in customary black except for a strip of exposed skin around the eyes, is balanced on the heel of one foot atop a naked katana thrust between the stones of the path. The pose is so damn cool you just stop walking and stare.

The ninja reaches behind his back and pulls out a small chalkboard. Without swaying, he begins writing on the board.

His handwriting sucks, so you have to move closer to read it.

You must be lost.

"Not really."

He smears it clear with a hand, chalk dust drifting down to lighten his uniform.

Only lost boys are found beyond this point. So, you must be lost to go farther.

"Does losing a boy count?"

The ninja scratches his head, which soon looks like he has dandruff. *I don't know.*

You attempt to walk past the ninja, but he leaps down from the sword and blocks your way.

"Why can't you speak?"

He pulls down the cloth covering his mouth and parts his lips. Inside it's all rusty red without any tongue. He starts writing on the chalkboard again. *Because I said something terrible I lost my tongue and have been posted here.*

"What did you say?"

The ninja just shakes his head sadly.

You set the backpack on the ground, ready to have a long argument with him over why he needs to let you pass when you hear the *clink!* of glass — the jar of preserved eel. Which makes you think of the apprentice pirate wanting to get his fake leg, which makes you think...

"If I found you a new tongue would you let me pass?" you ask him.

Agreed.

You get the jar and unscrew the top. You have to twist your hand about inside, not as easy as it looks, to get your fingers around the last eel. It's slippery and so cold. But finally you have it out and hold it before the ninja.

His hands move so fast you don't see him grabbing the eel from you. Only a breeze that chills the remaining slime on your palm. As he leans his head back and opens his blood-stained mouth, you're sure he's going to swallow the eel, but no, he drops it in and puffs his cheeks like he's swishing mouthwash.

Then: "Ah, that's so much better." The voice...it's so familiar. Adrian's, though the ninja lacks his bulk.

"You're welcome," you say.

"All lost boys have to go through the Gate. I can lead you to it but I can go no farther."

The Gate

Resembles Neil's bedroom closet door

down to the taped poster of the black-and-white *The Invisible Man*, his favorite movie. A pale green lichen has overgrown the poster's title lettering.

You remember sitting on the floor beside Neil late at night as the television flickered and Claude Rains unwrapped his head, the bandages revealing everything and nothing at once. You leaned your head on Neil's shoulder, distracting him so you could steal the bowl of popcorn from his lap. Buttered, salted kernels went flying. He laughed, though, and so you pushed him down to the carpet, your fingers slipping between his and the thick shag. He looked up at you. Half his face was lit by the television. One eye bright, the other dark. Everything and nothing at once. Conscious of his body beneath yours, of how his weak squirms were almost too much to bear, you felt scared, as if kissing him would be inviting disaster.

But you did.

Fine hairs tipped with luminescent beads rise from the lichen when your hand reaches for the doorknob.

"Looks deadly to the touch," the ninja says. He's actually been really chatty the last hour or so you've been walking towards the Gate. Just rambling about how good it will be to taste sushi again. He's also too curious about the pirate — you might have mentioned where you got the eel from — asking whether or not you think he could take her in a fair fight. And if she's pretty.

You're looking forward to losing him.

You take *Poisonous Lichens and Mosses of North America* from the backpack. Your finger traces a chart. Yes to glowing. Yes to eerie. No to blood-red. No to any skulls lying around.

Ephebus criminalis. You struggle to read the fine print by the lichen's glow. "Physical contact with this lichen can be hazardous to the remorseful," you read aloud.

"I think that's both of us." The ninja rubs his chin.

"You're afraid?"

He nods and backs away, lost to darkness.

"I'm not," you lie.

You thrust your hand at the door. Your fingers wriggle through what feels like a bath of acid and glue. Your worry that while turning the knob your wrist will crack, your hand fall off, swallowed. But you don't let go.

And when the Gate opens, you're shocked not to see Neil's room or even his house. No, ahead of you is the hall of lockers from school. B-Wing, the very hall where Neil's locker is.

The Lockers

Are just another kind of closet.

As you walk the darkened hallway, every locker door begins to tremble. You look to your left and see fingertips sliding through the gratings at the very tops of the metal doors. You look to your right and see eyes watching you from within the lockers.

"Neil?" you call out.

Laughter, not giggling but cruel and coarse laughter, comes from the lockers.

"Who's there?"

Down the hall, from around a corner, steps Neil. His head hangs down, gaze kept to the scuffed floor tiles, his arms hanging limp. He shuffles a bit farther before sitting down cross-legged in the intersection.

You call out his name again.

He shakes his head.

You start to run toward him. Then the lockers rattle so hard that their doors must soon burst.

Over the din you hear Neil's muttering clear, as if he stood behind you, whispering in your ear. "They'll talk about me. They'll stare at me. And laugh at me."

"Neil."

He dips his head, chin tight against his chest, and wraps his arms around himself. "They'll talk about me. They'll stare at me. And laugh at me."

Seeing him so hurts worse than the lichen. "Is that what Adrian told you?" You have to scream the question because of the noise. You reach him and collapse next to him.

He nods.

You remember the kids who teased you in junior high. They thought you were different. Not different in crazy, wonderful ways, how you felt when you ran around so hard you could collapse exhausted but laughing, or while captivated by the adventures of cartoon heroes. No, they wanted you to feel less than them, even though you breathed the same as them, stuffed food into your mouth in the cafeteria like everyone else. You learned to ignore them.

You slip your hand under his. You ignore the next bout of laughter from the lockers. "You can't hide away forever. Even after high school, there may be people who'll stare when I hold your hand," you say, though the words make your mouth taste bitter. You rest your lips against the top of his head. "Or when I tell you how much I love you. No matter what they say, you have the choice to listen or not."

Neil lifts his head a little.

"You can listen to them or listen to me."

You slide your face down, your mouth pressing first against his forehead, then the tip of his nose before coming to stop so close to his parted lips.

"You said you love me," he whispers.

Those lockers have hushed. Or maybe you're no longer paying attention to them.

"I know," you say. You feel breathless and weary yet eager for the next moment.

He kisses you. You might be surprised...maybe not, but you almost lose the kiss to the smile you begin as you stare into his wide-open eyes.

Together, you stand.

The Gate is still ajar and you lead him back through it, stepping over a pile of gauze bandages — Neil's last Halloween costume — and stacks of wool sweaters, past a couple of fishing poles. Shirts hanging in the way are pushed aside until

you emerge into Neil's bedroom, where it's bright. Saturday morning streams in through the windows.

"I'd love to make you breakfast. Even if you aren't hungry," you tell him.

He laughs and nods.

"But," he says, "before we do anything else, I need your help."

Working together, your arms often brushing against one another, you start removing the pins from the hinges of his closet door.

Acknowledgments

MY THANK YOU LIST (IN NO ORDER THAN what came to mind in the a.m. hours without much caffeine in my bloodstream):

Thank you, Holly, for teaching me to appreciate the intricacies of young adult fiction and reminding me it's a genre of "firsts."

Thank you, Alex, for all the support, all the beauty of words on the page and of the page. And the chiding.

Thank you, editors — Brit Mandelo & Julia Rios & An Owomoyela; Matt Cresswell; Ellen Datlow & Terri Windling; Sean Wallace & Jack Fisher — for believing in my stories enough to include them in so many fine books and magazines.

Thank you, many illustrators, who toiled away trying to bring solidity to my notions, not an easy task.

Thank you, Mom, for all the delicious calories and for challenging my shirt and waistband sizes.

Thank you, Ann, for always knowing what a story needs and when it needs it. And for telling me these secrets.

Thank you, Will and Aimee and Casey and Joe and Daniel, for knowing that writing is so lonely that sometimes you need to talk to a dear friend.

Thank you, pharmaceutical industries, for giving me so much in such little tablets to write about. If only I could pronounce the medications' real names.

Thank you, Syfy Channel, for making me realize that, no matter how bad I may feel about my own writing, I need only watch one of your "original pictures" to be reminded I'm better than *Bearantula Attacks*.

And thank you, reader, who bothered to turn to this page, and keep reading down to these words, when clearly the last of the stories in this book was over. You get a gold star. It will be in the mail.

Credits

About the Author

STEVE BERMAN SURVIVED BULLYING IN high school (you can, too). He came out as gay many years ago. He collects plush monsters. His favorite holiday is Halloween. He has viewed stars in the clearest of skies, on the steppes of Mongolia. His novel *Vintage: A Ghost Story* was a finalist for the Andre Norton Award. He resides in New Jersey, the only state in America with an official devil.

CPSIA information can be obtained at www.ICGtesting.com
Printed in the USA
BVOW07s1450100914

366291BV00004B/187/P